Par... at Your Fingertips

Joni Wood

iUniverse, Inc.
Bloomington

Paradise at Your Fingertips

Copyright © 2012 by Joni Wood.

This is a work of fiction. All of the characters, names, incidents, organizations, and dialogue in this novel are either the products of the author's imagination or are used fictitiously.

iUniverse books may be ordered through booksellers or by contacting:

iUniverse
1663 Liberty Drive
Bloomington, IN 47403
www.iuniverse.com
1-800-Authors (1-800-288-4677)

ISBN: 978-1-4759-0108-5 (sc)
ISBN: 978-1-4759-0110-8 (hc)
ISBN: 978-1-4759-0109-2 (ebk)

Printed in the United States of America

iUniverse rev. date: 04/05/2012

Contents

Prologue

The trees, the lake, the hills, the paradise, you can feel it at your fingertips. You breathe in the air, it's fresh. You look out at the water, it's clean. You put your arms out and you embrace this piece of paradise and say to yourself, it's all mine. But of course reality sets in and your attention is brought back into focus. The real world of drudgery! Paperwork, phone calls and e-mails! Work is no paradise.

Life has a funny way of bringing your focus back into reality. If only paradise was at your fingertips, you know you can feel it, it's out there somewhere. It's like going to a place with your true love without a care in the world. We all dream about it. For some of us this means being on a deserted island with your lover who finds you irresistible and who pleases you in ways that you never even thought of. While for others this might mean some long awaited down time with nothing but peace and quiet while reading a good book and being wrapped up in a life that is free from the drudgery of everyday life. Twenty years ago, I may have longed for the first scenario but today I think the second is more to my liking.But life is all about going to work, doing everything for the kids, walking the dog, listening to the drums and preparing lunches, dinner and doing laundry day in and day out. All these mundane jobs of everyday life never seem to end.

My *Tante (Aunt in Dutch)* Wilma once told me, "Jeanette, love can be complicated but if you simply respect each other and have open communication and great sex in your marriage, you will do fine."

Now, I blushed when she told me this, since I was only fourteen years old at the time. I kind of understood what she meant but I was a bit naïve at the time. I started thinking about marriage vows. *What does the I do mean anyway? Maybe I do now but maybe I don't want to later,* I thought to myself. *Now that's not good to think that way and that's how you end up in divorce.*

What about the, in sickness and in health, for richer or poorer, until death do you part really mean? I ask myself. We all seem to understand the *until death do you part*, that usually happens when you are old and everyone hopes for the richer part instead of the poorer part but it's the sickness part that you don't really think about when you are young. I'm not talking about colds, measles and flu but the ugly kind of sickness like when you find out that your husband has a tumour the size of a grapefruit sitting on the inside of his stomach that is literally sucking the life out of him. It's hard to believe. *How can this be? He is only forty-eight years old,* I ask myself. "His blood pressure is too low. I think he's bleeding internally," says my family doctor. "He needs a blood transfusion and he needs it today. He failed his physical." "Pardon me?" I ask in disbelief. *What did I just hear?* I ask myself. It's like someone kicking you as hard as they can in the stomach and knocking the wind right out of you. The panic sets in and you can't breathe. *Tumour means cancer and that means death, so how do I get through this crisis?*

Somehow, I muster up the strength to take him to the hospital and spend the six hours in the Emergency Department for tests only to be refused the very blood transfusion that he so desperately needs. The doctors at the hospital don't want to mask the problem until they find out what is really causing his hemoglobin to drop so much. So by now I'm confused and upset because we are told to come back the next day for more tests and in the meantime if things get worse, we are told not to hesitate to bring him back. "Go home?" I question. "It's one-thirty in the morning. Aren't you going to keep him overnight to be on the safe side? He's bleeding internally, don't you know?" The answer I hear is, "No, I'm sorry we don't have enough beds; please bring him back in the morning."All that went through my mind at that moment is how all the government cutbacks don't really affect you until a time like this. Now instead I go home disillusioned, try to sleep, get up exhausted and come back the next day for round two of tests and more waiting and not knowing what's wrong and what to expect next. Oh, how I long for a little piece of paradise. I would even settle for mundane duties at this time but instead my sleep is interrupted and my thoughts are jumbled and my heart is heavy.

CHAPTER ONE

The Early Years

Being born a twin is most fascinating. My sister and I started off together in a tiny little room squished inside our mother's womb. We were born eight minutes apart, weighing four pounds, seven ounces and four pounds, one ounce each respectively. Together we weighed the same as one baby would and since Maria was born first, this made her the dominant one. She never let me forget the fact that she was older than me, even though it was by eight lousy minutes.

"Respect your elders," she said to me from the time she could first talk and point her finger at me. She seemed to like ordering me around and she always said that she had every right to do so just because she was older.

Even though Maria was dominant, I think you form a special bond being a twin that is always there no matter what happens in life. There were times throughout our lives when we were not physically together but the bond we had always remained strong. The joys and the sorrows of growing up with someone the same age was both a pleasure and a pain. I must say, I never felt lonely while growing up and I always had my best friend with me wherever I went. This made me feel good until the times when she would beat me up out of fits of jealousy and make me feel bad.

"He's no good for you," Maria said to me. "How can you kiss him in the woods?"

"I didn't kiss him, he kissed me," I explained to Maria. "He's actually a really good kisser."

"That's gross," she said. "You can do better than him. You should dump him."

"Okay, I will," I said reluctantly. I didn't want my sister to think that I was easy but I was only in grade five at the time and it was all innocent but who knew where it would lead to. Don Bentley had written all about me in his diary and brought it to school one day. I think he intended only to show me what he wrote but Mike Grave saw the book, took it out of his hands and started to read out loud all of the personal thoughts about me. It was a little embarrassing to have everyone in the hall snickering as Mike started to read from the diary in a high-pitched mocking type of voice.

Oh Jeanette Vandermeer, you are so beautiful. I think about you all the time. I want to be with you forever. I hope today is the day that you will say that you love me too.

When I heard these words spoken about me, I wanted to crawl under a rock. Everyone started to laugh as Don wrestled with Mike to get his diary back. I liked Don but felt a little sorry for him at the same time since he was new to our school and he didn't have many friends. When he asked me to meet him after school in the woods, I wasn't sure what to think but I went anyway. When I got there, all he wanted to do was kiss me. I wasn't sure how to react but I liked it so I didn't stop him. That's when Maria showed up. She had followed me into the woods, gave me a disgusted look and told Don to go home.

At the time, I thought that she was being protective of me but later on I realized that she was just jealous that I had a boyfriend who was interested in me and she did not. After that incident, I decided not to even acknowledge Don as my boyfriend in front of Maria so that I wouldn't make her feel bad.

My Mom and Dad used to say that we were like night and day. Even though we grew up in the same household and had the same values impressed upon us, we were so different. My parents dressed us in the same clothes when we were little since we were twins and it looked cute. Needless to say, we were fraternal twins so we physically looked different even though we were always dressed the same. I was taller with dark wavy brown hair with a slim build while she was shorter with blonde curly hair with a stocky build.

We were so different in many other ways as well. Maria was witty, "Quick on the trigger," my Dad always said and outgoing while I wasn't funny in the least. I was quiet and shy and didn't understand all the jokes that were told but laughed out loud anyway to make it seem like I did. I liked school and studying while Maria didn't always go to school and never studied so when it came time for our report cards to come home from school there was always the calm before the storm. My parents praised me for my good marks and then I heard my father ask Maria, "Why can't you be more like your sister and do better in school?"

"I can't help it if she's smarter than me," said Maria.

"She's not smarter than you," my mother stepped in to say. "You can do better if you just put in more of an effort Maria."

"I hate school," Maria shouted and then she ran to her room and slammed the door.

I went into our room to try to console her but as usual, Maria was in one of her moods and there was nothing I could do or say to make her feel better. She told me to get out as she belted me on my way out of our room.

We were both athletic but in different ways. When we played soccer, Maria was like a tank and kicked the ball hard and bulldozed her way down the field. I was more of a finesse player and I handled the ball with skill and precision. Maria was always jealous that I scored more goals than she ever did in a game. Again she would belt me in the arm when I wasn't looking.

"Hey, what was that for?" I asked as I rubbed my arm.

"That's for the next time you do something that bugs me," she said as she stomped away.

Even though we were so different, there was a certain connection that I had with Maria that gave us a special bond. I could feel her pain in her times of anguish and I always tried to help her out even after she was mean to me. I understood that although we were so different in our personality and style, the real difference between us was in the way we felt inside while growing up. I was happy and she never really seemed to be.

Even at a very young age, Maria showed signs of unhappiness. At our first birthday party, my mother had baked each of us our own cake. She had decorated each one with hearts around the edges and a smiley face in the middle but she personalized them by piping each of our own names onto our individual cakes. After Maria finished her slice of cake, she didn't seem to be satisfied with just one piece and she reached over from her high chair and grabbed my piece of cake. My Mom swiftly said, 'NO!' to Maria and strapped her in her seat. She was startled and began to cry which in turn made me cry also. Then Maria began to bang her fists on her high chair and she shouted, "NO, I want more!" My father was recording her tantrum on his video camera at the time and every year on our birthday they would show the same footage of the events. For years everyone laughed except for Maria who would just grumble every time they showed it.

While growing up, I noticed that Maria's irritability could be triggered by the smallest of things. In the morning she used to eat her bowl of corn flakes that she placed right in front of the cereal box so that no-one could look at her while she ate. When I peeked at her from behind the box while she was eating, she shouted, "What are you staring at?"

"Nothing," I said as I smiled at her. "Just wondered how you were doing this morning."

"Well, leave me the fuck alone," Maria said as she stomped away to her room to hide from the world for a while. Since we shared a room, it meant that every time while she was in one of her bad moods, I couldn't go in there. I never knew how long these moods would last. It could be for hours or even days.

Suddenly, as if nothing had ever been wrong, Maria came out of our room to ask me if I wanted to play a game of tennis. I simply responded with a nod and I was happy that she was in a better mood once again.

My little brother Ronald also seemed to get under Maria's skin about the smallest of things. I could see that he was too young to understand her mood swings and he would do things that would bother Maria. He used to call her names like *Buster Brown* and take her cigarettes from her and run away from her laughing. When she caught up to him though, she was so enraged that she beat him up until he cried. I had to be the one to rescue him from her and physically pry her from hurting him any further.

"Why don't you leave him alone," I yelled at Maria. "He's only little and I think he's just trying to tell you to quit smoking."

"He's just a little shit and he should leave my stuff alone," she said.

I think my sister's attitude had a lot to do with these mood swings that grabbed a hold of her at a very young age. I found her shifts in mood to be difficult to deal with at times but it was the physical swings that followed that hurt the most. It always looked like she tried so hard to fight the evil moods that lurked inside but most of the time it seemed to me that she was losing the battle. If only my parents knew that these mood swings were not normal teenage behaviour and that she needed help, things could have turned out differently. There was a reason also why my oldest brother Matt left the house when he turned eighteen but at the time I was only ten years old and had no idea why.

It was my other brother Mark who introduced Maria to smoking pot when she was only twelve years old. He tried to get both of us to try it.

"Hey Rita Retards," said Mark. "Do you two want to try smoking some really good stuff?" I watched as he pulled out some rolling papers and a sandwich baggy full of weed from his pocket and skillfully started placing it on the paper. He then rolled it up into a *spiff* as he called it, licked it and then lit it.

"Not me! That stuff makes you crazy," I said to Mark.

"Don't be retarded Jeanette," said Mark. "It won't hurt you. Just have a toke."

I didn't want anything to do with drugs so I ran away from him but Maria stayed and tried a toke from the joint. Later she told me how great it made her feel and that I didn't know what I was missing.

Maria was always getting herself into deeper trouble with all the choices that she made and sometimes these choices got me into trouble as well. When we went together to *Ontario Place* in *Toronto* to see a *Cheap Trick* concert, she had brought some pot and smoked up before we entered the show. What I didn't realize was that the police were watching us from a distance and suddenly they approached us and escorted both of us down to the police station that night. When my father was called by the police to pick up his girls from the station, I could see that he was furious with us. He grabbed each of us by the scruff of the neck and directed us to get in the car. On our way home, all he did was swear at us over and over and told us not to say a word.

"God damn it! What's the matter with you two? You Maria I can understand but you Jeanette, I can't," he shouted at us. "All that your mother and I have done for you and this is how you repay us?"

This made me feel terrible. He had expected this type of behaviour from Maria but not from me. At that point, I didn't have the heart to tell him that it was just Maria who smoked the pot and that I was just there with her. I didn't mind taking some of the blame though if it meant that my father wouldn't be so hard on Maria.

"Why didn't you snitch on me and tell him that you didn't even smoke any dope Jeanette?" said Maria.

"I don't know. You know how Dad can be," I said. "I thought it would be better for you to be grounded with me so that way we can at least still hang out together."

"You're so retarded Jeanette but thanks for sticking by me," said Maria.

After that incident, Maria gravitated toward all the dope heads at school and she started to skip school on a regular basis. She got into fist fights with the boys and got suspended for fighting. This is when she got the nickname *Butch*.

I was so embarrassed that she was my sister so I started hanging out with different friends at school. At home, I tried to advise Maria that I thought she was getting out of control and that she should think about the consequences of her actions. She didn't seem to care about what I had to say to her. It was when I saw her steal money from my mother's purse that I told her that she had crossed the line.

"How can you do that Maria?" I asked her. "You had better put that money back."

"Shut up Jeanette," answered Maria. "I just need some extra cash to buy an ounce. It's no big deal. She won't miss it."

"How can you say that?" I asked her in disbelief.

"Shut up and leave me alone," said Maria as she tackled me to the ground and started throwing punches at me. Suddenly, I felt a sharp pain in my left cheek and I screamed out so loud that Maria stopped and looked at me in horror. In her hand was a pen dripping with blood that she had stabbed me with.

I don't think Maria even felt sorry at the time for what she did to me that day. When I came back from the hospital and tried to show her the stitches, she didn't even look up at me. She had an expressionless look on her face that said it all. I couldn't help but think that she needed something. She looked so lost.

When we turned fifteen, our family moved from *Mississauga, Ontario* to *London, Ontario* to start a new business. Our parents moved for economic reasons but they didn't even seem to consider how we may have felt about moving away from all of our friends at that age. Friends meant everything to a fifteen year old. I thought that somehow the move would be a good change for Maria though. Just maybe she would make some new friends and make a fresh start.

CHAPTER TWO

The summer of 1981

Maria and I each made our own new friends at our new high school in *London* but she was up to her same old habits of smoking pot and skipping school in no time at all. We didn't hang around each other very much at school since our interests were so different. The only time we spent together was when we had to work on the weekends at a deli-market in downtown *London*. After work Maria was always off to a party while I went home to relax after a long day at work. She did finally come up to me four years after she had hurt me though and said that she was sorry.

"Sorry for what?" I asked.

"For stabbing you in the face that day," she said. "I really didn't mean to do that. I don't know what got into me then. I can't explain it other than I feel just like *Dr. Jekyll* and *Mr. Hyde* sometimes."

"That's okay, I've forgotten all about that," I lied. Although the scar that was left on my face was minimal now, I was self-conscience about it being there in the middle of my cheek. Luckily, I could cover it up with make-up although I didn't like wearing a lot of it. "I'm just glad you didn't poke my eye out that day!"

As we finished high school, the summer of 1981 would prove to be the most adventurous summer that I ever had. Maria and I started planning a camping trip out west with our cousin, John deValk. For me, it was all about acting grown up and being free of school and parents for the first time in my life. For Maria, it was all about partying. Maria and I had just turned nineteen years old and our cousin was nineteen and a half. We were all young, confident and somewhat unattached. I thought I knew what life was all about but I would soon learn some life lessons along the way.

"So what else do you think we need to bring Maria?" I asked. "I have our camping supplies, a good map and money. I can't wait to go. There's only nine more weeks until we get to leave."

"I don't have any money left Jeanette," replied Maria.

"What have you done with all your money?" I asked.

"I fucking spent it all. Now I have to bag apples full time for eight weeks straight. I should be able to make enough money for the trip by then," said Maria.

"You don't have anything to show for all the money that you made at the deli this year Maria?" I asked. "I saved a thousand dollars for our trip and you went and spent all your money on drugs didn't you?"

"Shut up miss goody-two shoes," said Maria. "You know I like to party, besides I'll make it up by working full-time for the next eight weeks."

"Well, I hope you go crazy bagging apples for eight hours a day," I said. "That's the price you have to pay for being stupid and smoking all that dope."

Maria just gave me an evil eye look and grumbled as she didn't seem to have much to say at that point. The next day, she went off to work and had to start bagging apples while I was able to be at home, have fun playing tennis and making all the plans for our trip. That is when I met Richard Reinhardt and Maria met Larry Borden.

After work, Maria said to me, "Hey, Jeanette, you've been hanging around with Richard a lot lately."

"We're just friends. He is a good tennis player and since you're stuck bagging all those apples, I had to find a new tennis partner," I said. "What is it with you and that long-haired Larry guy? He seems a bit creepy to me."

"I met him at work. He's twenty-two and has an ex-wife and two year old daughter out west. He's here bagging apples just long enough to get enough money to travel back out there. I'm not dating him if that's what you're thinking Jeanette," answered Maria.

"He's used baggage Maria. You need to meet someone better than him," I said.

"Well, who's to say Richard is any better?" said Maria. He's a little dull don't you think?"

"I like him as a friend, that's all. We aren't dating either," I told Maria.

"Good," said Maria. "We need to be free of all the balls and chains on this trip so that we can have a blast!"

"I agree, we have to be free-birds, just like the song *Free Bird* by *Lynyrd Skynyrd*," I said to Maria.

"Hey, I put that song along with some *Neil Young* and *Genesis* on a cassette tape that I'm bringing in the car," said Maria. "Oh and I also put my all time favourite song, *Whole Lotta Love* by *Led Zepplin*, on that tape too," said Maria.

"Sounds like you got the choice of music all covered," I said to Maria. "I'm going to give John a call sometime soon to make sure he is on track for heading out west with us."

When I called my cousin John a couple of weeks later, I asked him, "Do you have enough money for the trip John? I figure we each need around a thousand dollars to cover the cost for gas, camping and food. You can bring extra money for any entertainment if you like."

"I've been working at *McDonald's* after school and on weekends and putting in a lot of extra hours so I should have enough in the next couple of weeks. If I don't fucking ever eat at *McDicks* again, I'll be happy Jeanette," said John. "What about you and Maria?"

"I saved enough from working at the deli and Maria has been bagging apples full time for the last six weeks and she should have a thousand bucks saved by the time we have to go," I said to John.

"Awesome! It'll be a great trip Jeanette. I'm glad your parents let us borrow their car for the two and a half month journey," said John. "That is really great of them to do that."

"Can you believe they trust us to go all that way and back? They never would have let Maria and I go together on this trip without you. I am so glad that they think you are a man now that will protect us. My Dad just changed the oil on the *Chevy Nova* and put new tires on it and gave it a tune-up so it should all be ready to go," I said.

"Hey, I am a man now. I'm not six-foot four and two-hundred and twenty pounds for nothing. I think it is a matter of safety in numbers too. Your Mom and Dad know that we will all stick together and watch out for each other. You're the smart one and I'm the strong one. I don't know about Maria though. Can we safely say she is the smooth-talking one?" asked John.

"I guess you could say that. If we get into any trouble along the way, I know she'll talk her way out of it," I replied. "She did inherit my Dad's charming personality and she's quick on the trigger as my Dad always says."

"Tell Maria that I got some really good *ganja* for the trip too," said John. "See you in a couple of weeks!"

John was a special cousin who was like a best friend to both Maria and I. We grew up with him living next door to us in *Deux Montanges, Quebec* most of our young life until he and his family moved to the *United States* to live in *Pittsburgh, Pennsylvania* and we moved to *Mississauga, Ontario*. The three of us were good friends who protected each other like we were part of a wolf pack. Even when John moved away at age ten, we still got together for all the holidays and spent our summers together. Now we were getting prepared to head out on the biggest trip of our lives.

I was happy when Maria and I arrived safely in *Pittsburgh* after the eight and a half hour drive that I knew so well from our visits with my parents. This time though, it was a great feeling to have made the trip all on our own. I thought that Maria even handled the border crossing really well.

"What nationality are you both?" asked the border guard.

"Canadian," we each answered. Maria answered all the rest of the questions since she was the driver and I was relieved to let her handle it.

"Where are you headed?" asked the guard.

"To *Pittsburgh*," said Maria.

"What is your purpose for going there and how long will you be staying in the *United States*?" asked the guard.

"We are going for a visit to see my cousin and we are only staying one night and then we are travelling back into *Canada* to go out to the west coast after that to visit my brother who is stationed in the Navy in *Esquimalt, B.C.,*" said Maria.

"Did you bring anything into the country?" asked the guard.

"No sir just our clothes and some camping equipment," said Maria.

"Please hand me some identification and pop open the trunk," said the guard.

At this point I was getting a little nervous about what Maria had brought with her into the country that would be considered illegal. Maria complied with his requests and showed him her birth certificate and I showed him mine. Then Maria got out of the car and opened the trunk. While he rummaged through a few of our belongings I could hear some laughter but I couldn't make out what they were saying since I stayed in the car. After a few minutes the border guard smiled at me, waved his hand and sent us on our way.

"I hate crossing the border Maria," I said to her. "It makes me nervous. What were you saying to him?"

"He just asked me if we were planning to stop in *Jasper National Park* on our way out west and I told him that we were. He said he has an aunt and uncle that live near there in *Alberta* and it's so beautiful there. He has dual citizenship just like John does," said Maria.

"Well, I was sweating buckets sitting here in the car waiting. I didn't know what illegal substances you may have brought with you," I said to Maria.

"Relax Jeanette. You're such a worry wart," said Maria. "I only brought my favourite bong and it's stuffed down my pants. He won't get that."

"You're lucky he didn't strip search you," I said.

"Oh well, that could have been fun you know. He was cute," said Maria.

"Funny. Now what were you laughing about with him?" I asked.

"He told me that he was part American and part Canadian. I just asked him what he liked being best, a *Yankee Dog* or a *Canuck Goose*," said Maria as she laughed. "He just laughed and said that he was glad to be both a *Yank* and a *Canuck* which allowed him to live and work in both countries."

"Well, I'm glad you smoothed that one over," I said. "I'm surprised that he didn't think you were crazy and pull us over for a more thorough search."

"You don't have much faith in me do you little sister?" asked Maria. "You need to trust me more."

"Now that's a scary thought," I said. "I'll be glad once we pick John up in *Pittsburgh* and then get back into *Canada*."

After our stay with John overnight in *Pittsburgh,* we headed out on our way bright and early the next morning. My *Tante* Wilma had a few parting words for us.

"Be careful on the road and have a great time you three musketeers," she said. "Now make sure to keep your eyes on the road and stay on the trails when you get out west. Don't get eaten by any bears and do call us once in a while to let us know how you are doing. Just call collect, I don't care."

As she gave each of us a big hug, she stuffed one hundred dollars into each of our pockets and said, "Bon Voyage, wolf pack." I thought that my aunt was very generous to give us each some extra spending cash. I told her that it wasn't necessary to give us so much but she didn't want it any other way and just motioned for us to get on our way.

We all waved good-bye and Maria jumped in the driver's seat, popped her cassette tape into the player and turned the music up full blast. John and I got in the car and had big smiles on our faces as we looked at each other and shouted, "Yee-ha!" I was so excited about finally being on the first day of our trip together and Maria started to speed once she reached the highway. Both John and I told her to slow down but she didn't listen to us. As she kept speeding, we passed up a highway patrol car stopped at the side of the road. The police had pulled over a motorist and Maria rolled down her window and yelled out, "Another one bites the dust!" As Maria shouted this, the police officer stopped what he was doing, jumped in his patrol car and came after us.

"Ah, shit," said Maria. "His lights are flashing. What should I do?"

"Slow down and pull over to the side of the highway Maria," said John.

"What's the matter with you Maria?" I asked. "Do you think you can out run him in this car? You can't ever leave well enough alone can you?"

"Relax. I got it covered," said Maria.

My heart started to pound as all I could think about was that bong she had down her pants and the *ganga* that John had down his. When the officer approached the vehicle I could see that he stood around six foot four in height, had broad shoulders, very large hands and had a look of annoyance on his face. He asked for Maria's driver's license and registration of the car.

"What's the big hurry?" he asked Maria.

"Sorry officer, we are heading on a trip out west to *British Columbia, Canada* and this is the first day of our trip and I guess I wasn't really paying attention to my speed. It's such a nice day and the traffic isn't heavy at all. I realize now that I must have been going a tad over the speed limit," she said to him as she smiled.

"Well now, let me get this straight. You want me to believe that you didn't know you were speeding over the limit by twenty-five miles per hour?" asked the officer. "Anything more than ten miles per hour over the limit and I have the discretion to impound your vehicle on the spot. Instead, I am only going to write you up a ticket for going ten miles per hour over and fine you ninety dollars."

I could see Maria swallowing hard as she rolled her eyes. I hoped she would realize that she should count her lucky stars and just accept the situation and not try to argue with the police officer.

"Now will that be cash or *VISA*?" said the officer.

"Do you have a *VISA* machine with you in the car?" asked Maria.

"Yes ma'am. We carry it for convenience sake if people don't have enough cash on them. Since you are from *Canada* though, you can't leave until the fine is paid in cash or by *VISA*," he said. "By the way, what was it that you yelled at me out of your window? I couldn't hear what you said but I had to let the other people off the hook and come after you to find out."

"I said, '*Another one bites the dust*', as a joke," she replied.

"Well, I hope you realize now who bit the dust today," said the officer. Maria gave the officer the one hundred dollars that she got from my aunt to pay the fine. When the officer returned ten dollars to her, she cursed under her breath.

The officer said, "Thank-you and please slow down and have a safe trip."

When the officer returned to get in his patrol car, Maria got out of the car and ordered me to drive for the rest of the day to our first stop in *Michigan*.

"I hope you learned your lesson today Maria," said John.

"Fuck off John," said Maria. "That just cost me the equivalent of a good bag of weed."

"Well, I've got a good bag with me so we can smoke some when we get to camp," he said. "Maybe that'll make you feel better."

"You're damn right," said Maria. "Did you bring some beer too John."

"Of course I did Maria. I got all the bases covered," said John.

"What about dinner?" I asked. "Aren't you guys getting a little hungry?"

"I'm too pissed off to eat," said Maria.

"Well, I'm starving Jeanette," said John. "What are you going to make?"

"Your Mom packed us some steaks and I have some canned vegetables and some noodles," I said. "Does that sound good?"

"Great," said John as Maria only groaned and turned the music up louder. She was in one of her moods and it was always best to just leave her alone during these times. I knew it and John learned over the years to do the same.

CHAPTER THREE

Lake Superior Provincial Park— Old Woman's Bay

When we arrived at the first camp of the trip at *Bay City State Park* in *Michigan*, Maria set up our tents, although she still seemed to be in a bad mood, while John chopped up some firewood and I started making dinner.

"Thanks Jeanette. This steak sure beats eating wieners and beans," said John. "Where do you think we'll end up tomorrow? Did you look on the map?"

"I figure, we should be able to cross the border and make it to *Old Woman's Bay* at *Lake Superior Provincial Park* by dinner time tomorrow. We can stay there for a few days and relax and enjoy the area there," I said.

"I've heard so much about that park. It will be great to be back in *Canada* too," said John. "Maria, we will have to finish the weed tonight so that we don't bring any across the border. I think we have to play it safe so let's party."

"Now you're talking," said Maria. "The way my luck is lately, I don't think we should take the chance."

The next day we got up early and were on the road by eight in the morning. It only took us a few hours to reach the border. I was driving and told Maria to relax, that I would handle the border crossing this time. I was a little nervous anticipating what Maria and John had with them while we were going to cross the border.

"Did you guys finish smoking that entire bag of weed last night?" I asked John and Maria.

"Yes. There's no more left Jeanette, don't worry," said John.

"What about that bong Maria? Do you still have it?" I asked.

"Um, yes," she said.

"Give it to me," said John.

Maria complied with John's request and took the bong out of her pocket and gave it to him. He looked at it and then opened the window and threw it out as far as he could into the ditch along the highway.

"Hey, what was that all about?" asked Maria. "That was my favourite bong."

"You should never carry drug paraphilia across the border," he said. "If you get caught, you can go to jail. It's just not worth it. We can always buy another bong along the way. I have a friend in *Vancouver* who sells weed and all kinds of bongs."

"That sounds decent," said Maria. "I can't wait to go there."

"Let's keep everything smooth at the border," I said. "We are almost there."

When we arrived, there were only a few cars ahead of us. As we slowly approached the gate, I took a deep breath. The guard just asked me where we had been and where we were going. I told him that we came to the *United States* to pick up my cousin from *Pittsburgh* and now were headed out west. All he said to me was, "Have a nice trip."

"That was easy," I said to Maria and John.

"No sweat," said John. "You must have the face of an angel for him to just let us through like that. No offence to you Maria."

When I glanced over at Maria, I could tell that she was not pleased with John's comment since her face was flushed and she yelled, "Up yours John." She turned up the music louder while she just stared out the window for the rest of the day until we arrived at camp.

Once there, we had everything set up within half an hour. By now, we were getting really efficient at setting up camp. Before we ate dinner, I suggested that we hike along the rocky shores of *Lake Superior*. It was such a beautiful camp nestled in the woods along this great lake. I came to realize why this lake was not just one of the five great lakes but that it was superior in size and beauty to all the other great lakes. John ran up ahead of us along the bluff as Maria and I made our way up the hill. As we approached the top, we heard John's voice squeal in horror as it sounded like he slipped off the edge of the bluff. Then within four seconds, we heard a big splash in the water below.

Maria and I looked at each other in shock and ran to the edge of the bluff to see what had happened to John. All I could see were some ripples in the water. I then ran as fast as I could and Maria followed me to the bottom of the hill but I didn't see any sign of John.

"Do you see him anywhere?" Maria asked me.

"No," I said. "I don't see him at all."

21

Then all I heard next was a hysterical laugh coming from the top of the bluff. As I looked up, I could hear John laughing and I saw him pointing at us as he started to come down the hill.

"You should see the look on your faces," said John as he approached us holding his belly while laughing. "It's priceless."

"Oh John, you're such an asshole you know," said Maria. "I really thought you had slipped all the way down and fell to your death. You had better be careful when you go to sleep tonight. You might wake up dead after I'm done with you."

Maria started chasing after John and I started to laugh and then we all laughed so hard until it ached. The tension that was in the air had vanished. It was good to see Maria laughing as we went back to camp and I was happy that Maria was in a better mood.

"Holy crap John," I said. "That's one way to give us a heart attack you know."

"Sorry guys," said John. "I guess it was in bad taste but it sure as hell was funny."

"Let's eat," I said. "I'm starving and after that fiasco, I need a big glass of wine too."

That night as we were sitting around the campfire and I was enjoying another glass of wine and John and Maria were drinking a couple of beers, Maria pulled a small bong and a chunk of hash out of her pocket. As she put a piece of hash into the pipe and lit it, she exhaled and passed the bong to John.

"Where did you get that from?" asked John as he took a toke.

"I had an extra bong and some hash stashed away in the false lining of my luggage," said Maria.

"You're lucky we didn't have any problems at the border Maria," I said.

"No worries," said Maria.

"You are so lucky," said John as he took another toke and gave the bong back to Maria. "My sister and mother got strip searched one time right down to their bras and panties at the border."

"Wow," said Maria. "I can't believe that. What were they looking for?"

"Drugs, of course," said John. "Even though they were searched by female officers, they were so embarrassed by the whole ordeal."

"No doubt," I said. "Don't they need probable cause to strip search?"

"Sort of," said John. "At the time, they were looking for a certain mother daughter team of drug smugglers crossing the border and my Mom and sister fit the description of the smugglers. They were let go after they didn't find any drugs on them. They even had the dogs sniff around in their car but they came up empty."

The weather was beautiful while we stayed at this camp at *Old Woman's Bay*. We went on several more hikes and also walked along the beach along the shore of *Lake Superior* over the next few days. It was refreshing to feel the breeze from the lake brush against my face and I finally felt that I was starting to unwind.

John started the fire that night and at one point while Maria went to the washroom, my cousin commented to me, "Maria's mood seems to be a bit better now that we've been hiking and seeing some great views of the lake on our trip so far. She is so much like my brother Tim who has the same kind of moodiness. I'd almost think they could be twins."

"Yeah, I know," I said to him. "I think it's somewhat genetic from both of our mother's side of the family."

When Maria came back, she grabbed a beer and sat down with us around the fire.

"Do you guys remember the land that our parents bought up in *Crystal Lake* in northern *Ontario?*" asked John. "After we moved away, it was the one place that we could all get together and camp in the wilderness. We made our own outhouses and blazed our own trails."

"That was a lot of fun always when our families got together at the land but it sure sucked when we found out that we never actually ever owned the ten acres of land. It got sold to ten different people by a con-artist," said Maria.

"What ever happened to that guy?" I asked. "Did they ever catch him? My parents didn't say much after they paid him ten thousand dollars for the land and got ripped off. I think they were embarrassed being scammed by a charming guy like him."

"My parents were embarrassed as well but apparently this guy took off to Florida with approximately a hundred thousand dollars in his pocket and was never to be seen again," said John. "He was a very charming man as I remember him."

"Charming and conniving as I recall. Our parents were too trusting of people if you ask me," I said. "The only lesson we can learn from this is to never trust anyone with your hard earned money, no matter how charming they are and especially not from a guy with a name like Joe Smith."

CHAPTER FOUR

Spruce Woods Provincial Park

When we left *Lake Superior*, we travelled on the *Trans-Canada Highway* for what seemed like for ever before we reached the *Manitoba* border. The road was very hilly and the scenery beautiful. I didn't realize how far northern *Ontario* stretched until we drove for two days before reaching the border into *Manitoba*. We still had a long way to drive to reach the west coast but it was enjoyable to see the diverse landscape as we travelled on our way.

When we reached *Spruce Woods Provincial Park* near *Brando, Manitoba,* it was a very hot day. The park was interesting and unique in that it contained one of the very few areas of sand dunes in *Canada* called the *Spirit Sands*. Since it was a very hot day, we put on our bathing suits and headed for the lake for a swim. We found some rocks to dive off from and it felt good to cool down. John was the first one to dive in but he landed flat on his belly. Maria and I both dove off the rocks at the same time, side by side and landed in the water with precision.

"You guys look like synchronized divers," said John.

"You look like a red bellied sap-sucker," said Maria.

"Does it hurt John?" I asked.

"Yes, but I'm alright," said John. "My face is probably just as red as my belly though."

That night as we sat around the camp fire drinking our beer and wine, we reminisced about our life when we lived next door to each other in *Deux Montagnes, Quebec.*

"It's funny how we spoke *French* at school, had *English* friends in our neighbourhood and spoke *Dutch* at home when we grew up in *Deux Montagnes,*" I said.

"It was nice to know three different languages but I often got *French* and *Dutch* mixed up at school," said Maria. "I would start to speak *French* but ended up throwing *Dutch* words into the mix."

"I enjoyed speaking all those different languages," I said.

"Let's have a toke to the good old days," said Maria as she pulled out her hash and mixed it with some tobacco and rolled it into a spiff.

"I'll have a toke too," I said.

"What you?" asked Maria. "Are you sure you can handle it?"

"Let her have a toke Maria," said John. "Maybe she'll like it."

As Maria handed me the joint, I took a puff and held in the smoke for two seconds as Maria and John always did. I then blew out the smoke and coughed a little bit. At first I didn't feel anything from the toke so I decided to have another.

"That's enough for me. I'm going to the washroom so if I'm not back in five minutes, please send a search party out for me," I joked.

As I walked to the comfort station, I realized that I forgot to bring a flashlight with me and it was pitch black out. When I started to walk back to our campsite, I became disoriented and stopped in the middle of the road. I started to panic as I felt paranoid and was startled when someone tapped me on the shoulder and asked me, "Sont vous perdu?"

"Oui je ne peux pas trouver mon terrain de camping," I said in *French* to this girl. I must have looked a little lost standing there in the middle of the road without a flashlight. I told her that I couldn't find my campsite so she offered to help me find it. As we began to walk, we carried on a long conversation in *French*. She told me that she lived in *Brandon Manitoba* and came to this park to be at peace with the spirits that converged on the sands. I found it interesting to hear about her beliefs in the enchanted sand hills. She believed that spirits gathered at the *Devil's Punchbowl* that slid down a bowl-shaped depression forty-five metres deep and would then disappear into an ever-moving, eerie pool of blue-green water. She told me that it was a peaceful place to meditate. I told her that it sounded like a great place to visit.

When we arrived back to my campsite, I didn't see any sign of either John or Maria. I thanked the *French* girl for showing me the way back and asked her if she would be alright in finding her way back to her own campsite. She smiled and waved and disappeared into the dark night. Suddenly, I saw Maria and John appear from the distance as they approached me looking a little annoyed with me.

"Where have you been?" asked Maria. "We were sort of getting worried about you when you didn't come back after five minutes like you said that you would."

"I was site-seeing," I said.

"No really Jeanette," said John. "We started looking for you and thought we saw you but it looked like someone jumped into the bushes to hide from us. Was that you?"

"Yes, that was me," I said. "I thought you guys were hoodlums out to get me. I don't think I should toke anymore, it kind of makes me paranoid."

"I agree," said Maria. "It also makes you stupid. What were you thinking that we were hoodlums? We were out there for almost half an hour looking for you."

"I made a new friend," I said. "She's a *French* girl. She helped me back to my campsite when I got a little disoriented."

"What was her name?" asked Maria.

"I don't know," I said. "I never asked her and she didn't tell me. She invited us to come and visit the spirit sands at the punchbowl tomorrow."

"You're so retarded Jeanette," said Maria. "I don't know why Mark calls both of us Rita Retards; he should reserve that title just for you."

"Hey, that's enough. Leave her alone Maria," said John. "Anyone can get lost in a new camp all alone in the pitch dark of the night. Leave it to Jeanette to make a new friend and speak a different language while doing it."

"Thanks John," I said. "I'm exhausted so I'm going to bed now. See you guys in the morning."

The next morning as I was packing up our tent, the *French* girl came by to ask if we were going to go visit the spirit sands with her. I said to her that I would like to see it but that I didn't have much time since we were leaving that day. Maria and John said that they were not interested, so I left with the *French* girl and promised them that I would be back soon.

"My name is Jeanette Vandermeer. What is yours?" I asked her.

"Monique Mileux," she said rather proudly as she shook my hand. She was a pretty girl with beautiful green eyes, long black hair and high cheek bones. I could tell now in the daylight that she looked partly *Native-American*.

"*Merci* for helping me last night," I said to her.

"My pleasure," she said.

She spoke *English* rather well but had a *French* accent when she spoke. As we walked down a depression in the sand to the punchbowl, the air became cooler. Monique got down on her hands and knees, stuck her hand in the sand and picked out a rock. She then told me to do the same. As I rummaged around in the soft sand, I felt for a rock and picked one up from the sands that had a red tinge to it. Monique said I should hold the rock tight in my hand, close my eyes and make a wish while I was there. As I slowly closed my eyes, I felt a calm wind flow past my face. Then Monique told me that my wish would come true if I didn't reveal it to anyone. She also said that I should keep the rock with me at all times for good luck and that it would keep me safe on my journey. I thanked her for the whole experience and told her that I felt a feeling of peace and tranquility out here in the spirit sands. I waved to her as I headed back to camp to get back on the road again.

CHAPTER FIVE

Saskatchewan Landing Provincial Park

As we travelled to our next destination, *Saskatchewan Landing Provincial Park* located fifty kilometres north of *Swift Current, Saskatchewan*, I hung onto the spirit sand rock and felt excited about the journey that still lay ahead.

Before we drove north on the highway up to camp, we stopped in the quaint little town of *Swift Current* to pick up some supplies of food and ice for the cooler. While I was in the store, I also bought an awl and a piece of leather so that I could punch a hole in my spirit rock and tie the leather necklace around my neck for good luck.

As we travelled toward camp, out of nowhere, the *South Saskatchewan River* valley appeared suddenly. The landscape dropped off nearly one-hundred and forty-three metres down from the rolling hills above the river. It was a very enchanting place that looked spectacular in the evening as the sun fell down over the horizon. The sun was the biggest sun I had ever seen. It glowed bright red and appeared to be at least four times as large as the sun that I usually saw back home in *London*. The beauty of this area was something to see and remember.

"I can't get over how flat most of *Saskatchewan* is and then you find a place like this where the land just drops off way down into a valley of coulees," said John.

"It's as flat as piss on a plate out here and then these steep hills, razorback ridges and wooded ravines appear in the landscape," said Maria. "It's beautiful here."

"The sunsets here are amazing also," I commented. "It's interesting to see all of these different landscapes on our way out west. I can't wait until we reach the *Rocky Mountains* though. I've been waiting a long time to see the mountains up close."

"My roommate has been out west and said that it is spectacular when you see the mountains for the first time," said John.

"Who is that John?" I asked.

"That's Harold Vanier," said John. "He's a great guy. I've known him for a very long time. We went to middle school together and we are sharing an apartment now."

"Isn't he gay?" asked Maria.

"Yes he is," said John. "It's no big deal."

"Doesn't that bother you what people might think of you living with a gay guy?" I asked John.

"Not really," said John. "I don't give a shit what people think. He's a good friend and that's all that matters to me. Whenever I bring girls home, I never have to worry about him stealing them away from me do I?"

"That's true," said Maria as she laughed. "What about his boyfriends? Don't you worry they might find you more attractive and come onto to you John?"

"Shut up, will you Maria?" asked John.

Joni Wood

I thought that Maria had a valid point though. It was kind of weird to me to think that he lived with a gay man but that he himself wasn't and that it didn't bother him what people thought about him possibly being gay. I never heard John talk about having any specific girlfriend and whenever there were girls around, he always seemed to be a bit shy and awkward around them.

"Do you have a girlfriend at home John?" I asked.

"Not right now," said John. "What about you Jeanette. Do you have any special boyfriends?"

"Well, I met a guy named Richard Reinhardt but he's more of a friend than a boyfriend," I said.

"What about you Maria?" asked John.

"I met this guy Larry Borden but he's been married and divorced already and was planning to go back out west to visit his young daughter and ex-wife in the fall," said Maria. "So by the time we get back east, he'll be heading out on his way out west. There's probably not much hope in that ever working out for me."

"Well, let's have a drink to our freedom that we have now," said John as he raised his bottle of beer up in the air and clinked our drinks. "To all of us free spirits here today! May we all find love one day but for now, let's just party!"

"I'm with you John," I said as I held up my glass of wine and clinked with his bottle of beer and Maria's as well.

"Me too," said Maria. "Let's party!"

CHAPTER SIX

Banff National Park

The next day, I woke up a little hung over but managed to get up early anyway and got John and Maria ready to head back on the *Trans-Canada Highway* to *Banff National Park* in *Alberta*. The anticipation to see the *Canadian Rockies* was high and as we drove closer my excitement grew. The foothills slowly appeared from the distance as we entered the *Alberta* border. I could see the *Rocky Mountains* suddenly appear in grandiose form beyond the foothills. The mountains looked a lot larger in person than it ever did on television or in magazine pictures.

When we arrived in *Banff National Park*, there was so much to see and do. We decided to take the *Banff Gondola* up to the top of *Sulphur Mountain* to a level of twenty-two hundred and eighty metres above sea level. There was an outstanding view of the town of *Banff* waiting for us from the top if we trekked up the rest of the way up the mountain to the summit. I had brought my purse with me on the gondola ride not realizing that there was a hiking trail at the top where the gondola dropped us off. My cousin John laughed at me when he saw that I had my purse with me.

"I can't believe you brought your purse with you Jeanette. Do you still want to hike all the way up while carrying it with you?" asked John. "That thing looks like it would be awkward to carry on a hike."

"Leave it to Jeanette," said Maria. "You never go anywhere without your purse. *Banff Sulphur Mountain* conquered by the bag lady."

"You are so funny Maria," I said sarcastically. "I honestly would have left my purse back at camp had I realized we would be hiking further up the mountain today. I'm still going to make it to the top and nothing will stop me from going all the way up there. Not even this stupid heavy purse."

It took us nearly two hours to make the climb up but the view up there was fantastic. You could see all the various mountain peaks in a beautiful three hundred and sixty degree panoramic view. As we descended from the summit, it only took us one hour to hike back down. When we reached the bottom of the mountain, we decided to go to the hot springs of *Lake Louise* in *Banff* to relax in the comfort of the spa and I enjoyed the pristine beauty that surrounded us.

Next, we travelled nearby to the *Valley of the Ten Peaks* at *Moraine Lake*. Here the scenery was breath-taking as well. The long trip over several weeks was all well worth the experience that the west had to offer. We saw several black bears, a moose and bighorn sheep along the way. We took many pictures in front of cascading waterfalls, breathtaking views of the mountains and the brilliant turquoise blue lakes that surrounded the area.

We only made one wrong turn the next day when we went sight seeing by car and turned off the highway and headed up an old logging road that led us up a mountain side. The road looked like a shortcut on the map but we ended up half way up the mountain where a scraggily-haired old hillbilly stood in the middle of the road pointing a shot gun at us. He motioned for us to stop and get out of the car.

"Where do *y'all* think you're going?" asked the hillbilly who had no front teeth.

"I think we are lost," I said. "We'll go back and get out of your way."

"Let me see what you got first," he said.

He made us empty our pockets and took our pocket change and he stole Maria's bong. Luckily, I had hidden the majority of our paper money in the trunk of the car and the hillbilly only took a small amount of money that we each had on us.

"Now get and don't come back before my *itching* finger gets any *itchier*," he said.

After hearing that invitation to leave, I motioned to John and Maria to get back in the car and we fled down the mountain as fast as the car would go. I squeezed my spirit sand rock tightly in my hand and thought to myself, *I'm so glad that I made that wish to be safe on this trip at the spirit sands and that it is coming true.*

"Holy fuck," said Maria. "That guy scarred the shit out of me."

"Me too," said John. "And he had that shot gun pointed at me the whole time."

"Let's not wander off the beaten path anymore," I suggested as I laughed nervously along with John and Maria.

CHAPTER SEVEN

Jasper National Park

After the awful experience with the hillbilly near *Banff*, we stayed on the main roads and highways for the rest of the trip and didn't venture off to explore any unknown territory. We made our way to *Jasper National Park*. Here we walked up to view the *Athabasca Glacier* which was huge in size stretching six kilometres long, covering an area of six square kilometres and measuring up to three hundred metres thick in some sections. We also hiked up *Mount Edith Cavell* and had a close up view of the north face of the mountain after a short hike to *Cavell Meadows*.

When I called home to let our parents know that we had finally safely reached *Jasper National Park*, they told me that they were glad to hear my voice but that my brother Mark had called. He was stationed in the navy in *Esquimalt* in *British Columbia* and he wanted us to give him a call as soon as possible since he had a surprise for us but we had to get to *Vancouver* in two days to find out what that was.

"How's the trip so far Jeanette?" asked Mark when I called him that night.

"Awesome! We are having a great time," I said to Mark. "A few minor bumps along the way but otherwise everything is going great. So what's the big surprise that Mom was talking about that you have for us?"

"I can't tell you what it is yet other than I need you guys to get here no later than seven o'clock on Saturday night," he said.

"We were planning to stay here in *Jasper* for a few more days since it's so beautiful but if you insist, we'll get going tomorrow morning and we should be in *Vancouve*r to meet up with you by Saturday night."

"See you then Rita," said Mark. "Have a safe trip and don't be late."

When I told Maria and John that we had to leave in the morning to see Mark and that he wanted us to get to *Vancouver* by Saturday night, they seemed a little disappointed to leave *Jasper* since we had just arrived here and there were more hikes to go on.

"We can always stop here again on our way back home and stay longer to hike in the area then," I said to them.

"Well, whatever the surprise is, it better be good," said Maria.

"I sure hope it's worth it," said John. "Knowing Mark though, it will be good."

When we got to the *Vancouver* area, I called Mark and told him that we were going to set up our camp at *Golden Ears Provincial Park* near *Maple Ridge* in *British Columbia* and that we would meet him in *Vancouver* for dinner.

"What's the big surprise?" I asked.

"Come for dinner at six and I'll let you guys know then," said Mark.

When we arrived at the *Boathouse Restaurant* in downtown *Vancouver* I saw Mark sitting with his friend and colleague Eddie Burkoff.

Immediately my heart skipped a beat as I gazed at Eddie sitting there with Mark. He was so very handsome in his naval uniform with his short dark hair and overall good looks. His dimples appeared when he smiled my way.

"Hey you guys, over here," said Mark as he waved to us to come over to the table that he had reserved for five. *At least there's no girlfriend place setting here at the table*, I thought to myself.

"Nice to see you again Mark," said John. "It's been a long trip but a good one so far."

"Good to see you too John," said Mark as he shook his hand. "This is my buddy Eddie Burkoff and this is my cousin John deValk and my sisters Maria and Jeanette."

"My pleasure," said Eddie as he looked at each of us and smiled.

As we sat down, I didn't say much of anything to anyone but could only feel my focus drawn to Eddie. He was so cute and he kept smiling and looking at me while we ordered our food and as we ate. I asked myself a question that I was scarred to answer at this time, *Could this be instant love?*

John and Maria began telling Mark and Eddie all about our adventure so far including our brush with that crazy hillbilly up on the mountain and I just listened and laughed and had a good time.

"What about you Jeanette?" asked Eddie later on after we finished eating. "What was your favourite part of your trip so far?"

All I could think of at that moment was that my favourite part was *now* but I managed to say to him, "Conquering *Sulphur Mountain* while carrying my purse all the way to the top has to be my most memorable moment so far. That hike was rugged but the view from the summit was just fantastic." Maria and John laughed as I explained the story about hiking while carrying my purse.

"I've hiked there too, although not with my purse of course. The view is the best from the very top. I'm glad that you didn't let any purse stop you from seeing that great view," replied Eddie. "Has Mark told you guys where we are headed tonight?"

"We don't have a clue," said Maria. "Where the fuck are we going Mark?"

I didn't care where we were going as long as Eddie was coming with us.

"I've got tickets for everyone to see *Ozzy Osborne* on the *Crazy Train* tour with *Motorhead* being the opening act," said Mark. "How does that sound?"

"Wow, that sounds awesome Mark," said Maria.

"Cool," said John.

"Are you guys coming with us as well?" I asked Mark as I looked at Eddie.

"Yes we are," said Mark. "We had better get going. It should be a great concert."

When we left the restaurant, Mark told us to follow him to the *Vancouver Civic Centre* where the concert was to begin at eight that night. Before we entered the *Centre*, Maria and John smoked up and asked me if I wanted to as well. I hesitated but they convinced me that it was the best way to feel the full effect of the concert. I had a few tokes and it made me feel really mellow at first and we all laughed a great deal that night before the concert even started.

As I gazed at all the speakers on the concert floor standing from the floor to the ceiling, the music suddenly started with a roar and the sound felt like it was going right through me. The group *Motorhead* opened with their song, *The Ace of Spades*. All I felt were those words vibrating right through me. Then later, I heard *Ozzy* ask, "Are you ready *Vancouver* to board the *Crazy Train* tonight?" The crowd went wild as we all shouted and then *Ozzy* yelled, "All aboard, ha ha ha . . ."

The music was so loud that my heart felt like it was pounding to the beat of the music. It was a strange sensation and I started to feel faint from all the excitement. Eddie quickly put his arm around me to hold me up as he must have noticed that I looked a little pale. I was glad that he was there with me and it felt so good to be so close to him and to feel his arms around me, holding me tightly. Then suddenly, my mind went blank.

I didn't remember anything about the rest of the night until the next morning when I woke up and felt sick to my stomach. I quickly zipped open the tent and retched in the bushes nearby. I hoped that I didn't wake anyone up and when I focused my eyes on my watch, it read six fifteen in the morning. My head hurt and my mind was spinning as I stumbled back into the tent to lie down.

"What's going on?" asked Maria. "Are you okay?"

"I'm alright," I said. "Too much partying, I think."

"Go back to bed and sleep it off," said Maria.

I slept most of the day and as I got up in the late afternoon, I started to feel a little better but I wasn't feeling one hundred percent back to my normal self.

"Wow, that was some concert," I said to Maria and John.

"Yeah," said John. "And what was that with you and Eddie, Jeanette?"

"What are you talking about John?" I asked.

"Well, you two seemed to suck a lot of face at the concert until you passed out and we brought you back to camp," said John.

"Thanks. I don't remember anything about that," I replied as I blushed. "I like Eddie. He is so awesome."

"I hate to tell you Jeanette but Eddie was engaged and his fiancé broke it off only days before the concert," said Maria. "Mark was telling me that Eddie likes to play around and that's why she broke it off with him."

"You sound jealous," I said to Maria.

"Whatever. I just thought that you should know that he is probably rebounding right now," said Maria.

"Well, I can take care of myself, don't you worry about me," I said.

"Mark said we are invited to *Esquimalt* tonight to tour the ship," said Maria. "Do you want to go?"

"Yes but I don't think I am going to party so hard tonight though. I suddenly don't feel the greatest," I said.

That night, we ended up going to *Esquimalt* and had a barbeque on the beach by the ocean. It was refreshing to be at the beach with the light breeze that was coming off the water. My brother had bought some salmon and we cooked it over a bonfire at the spit on the beach. When we arrived, Eddie was there and he smiled and gave me a wink as I blushed. We had brought a salad and potatoes to add to the meal. We all had a few drinks and went to the ship for the tour after we finished eating.

When we went up the stairs onto the deck, there were several *Naval Officers* in uniform to greet us who offered us *navy double* drinks as they called them. They were very smooth drinks made from vodka and orange juice and some secret ingredient that seemed to make these drinks go down rather easily. I had a couple of drinks in total and still was not feeling well. I found myself running off to the side of the ship and when I got there, I heaved up over the edge and then plopped down on the deck of the ship. I sat there for quite some time before Eddie came by looking for me and asked me how I was feeling.

"Not the greatest. Must be those navy doubles and all that loud music from last night," I said. "My ears are still ringing from the concert."

"You have to sip those drinks slowly and yes the music was really loud but good," he said to me. He put his arm around me and helped me up. "Now, let's walk around to get you some fresh air to make you feel a little better."

"I'm alright, thanks," I said. "I think I need to go back to camp to have a good night's sleep. Are you still coming on the hike tomorrow at *Hell's Canyon?*"

"I'll be there, if you'll be there," he said as he winked at me. "Now let's get you on your way back to camp."

Eddie found Maria and John and suggested that they take me back to camp. When I woke up the next morning, I felt a little better but thought to myself that I had to stop this partying before it killed me. Being this hung over just wasn't worth the fun of all the nights before.

"You are such a lush," Maria said to me when she saw me get out of the tent in the late morning.

"Wow," I said. "I think I have to stop this madness and slow down. I don't know how you and John do this all the time."

"We're used to it, that's all. Eddie came by earlier this morning and wondered how you were doing," said Maria. "I told him you were sleeping so he went back to the base."

"I think I'm in love Maria," I said.

"He seems to be in love with you too," said Maria. "I don't know what you are going to do when we have to leave in a couple of days."

"I don't even want to think about that right now Maria," I said.

CHAPTER EIGHT

Voodoo

I was happy that I was able to see Eddie for a few more days before we had to leave to go back home. We all went together to *Hell's Canyon* on the last day of our stay and it was so beautiful there while we hiked in the majestic wilderness. Eddie and I were holding hands until I let go to have a closer look at how far down the gorge plunged. As I stepped under the railing and peered over the edge of the cliff, my footing slipped and I started to fall off the edge until Mark grabbed me from behind. He was able to hold onto my necklace which saved me from falling over the edge of the cliff. I nervously laughed as I gathered myself up from the edge and back onto the trail. I thanked Mark and held on tight to my lucky spirit sand rock as Eddie came over to me and wrapped his arms tightly around me.

"I'm glad you didn't plunge all the way down. I'm going to miss you Jeanette but I'll write to you every day once you get back home," said Eddie as he gave me a passionate kiss. "I'll come to visit you when I'm on my vacation break at Christmas time as well. Now promise me that you'll stay on the trail and have a safe trip back home."

I wanted to believe what he said to me but as I left to go back to camp that night, I missed him already and had an awful feeling that I would never see him again. As we arrived back at camp, Maria said that we were going to a bar to listen to some music for our last night in the *Vancouver* area. John led us to a run-down bar on *Davie*

Street in downtown *Vancouver* that was near the apartment of an old friend of his.

As we sat at a small table in the corner of the bar, John went to go visit his buddy, Jeremy Laxter who lived in the apartments next door. He told us that he was going to buy some pot from him and that we should wait in the bar until he got back in about an hour. When I looked around at all the people hanging out in this bar, I said to Maria, "This seems to be a really scummy place. I really feel uncomfortable here. I don't want to stay here very long."

"There's nothing to worry about Jeanette," said Maria. "You're always so paranoid."

"Have you noticed there seems to be a lot of gay couples here too?" I asked Maria as I gazed around and noticed several different same-sex couples arm in arm at the bar.

"Yup you're right. I think John is gay but he just doesn't seem to want to admit it to us," said Maria. "Once John gets back, I think we'll get the hell out of here. This place is starting to give me the creeps as well now."

After almost an hour, Maria and I decided to leave the bar to go find John next door. As we approached the apartment building, we saw John saying good-bye to his friend at the front door of his apartment. John gave his friend an awkward but passionate kiss on the lips. Maria and I looked at each other and quickly walked back to the street in front of the bar to wait for John.

"See, I knew it," said Maria.

"Let's not say anything to him Maria that we saw him," I said to her. "I don't think he saw us."

"Nope, you're right. My lips are sealed," said Maria.

As John turned the corner, Maria and I just acted as if we had just come out of the bar and were waiting for John to show up. John said hello to us and handed an orange bong to Maria.

"Here's a bong for you Maria," said John. "This is to replace the one I threw out into the ditch."

"Cool," said Maria. "Thanks a lot John."

That night when we got back to camp and John and Maria started to smoke some weed, I decided to go for a short walk to clear my head. I felt excited but disappointed as well about leaving the west coast to go back home. I liked it out here and I thought about how much I was going to miss Eddie but I was excited about the thought of starting University in a few weeks time when I got back home. My feelings seemed to be all mixed up.

My concentration was suddenly broken as I heard someone coming up from behind me. As I turned around to have a look, someone grabbed my arm, turned me around the opposite way and covered my mouth with some tape. As I tried to scream, my sound was muffled. My arms were bound and this someone was leading me away. I was terrified.

Then, in the next moment, I felt a scuffle and I was suddenly released. I then heard John yell,"Fuck off you asshole." He kicked this guy in the leg as hard as he could as he fled on foot. John took the tape off my mouth and asked me if I was alright.

"Yes, I think so," I said as I trembled. "What the hell just happened?"

"I'm not sure," said John. "I'm calling the cops."

Maria came running up to me and exclaimed, "Are you alright Jeanette?"

"Yes, I'm alright," I said as I gave her a big hug.

When the police arrived, we were told that there was a murderer on the loose who had been abducting and killing teenagers from camps in the greater *Vancouver* area. He was known as the *BC monster*. He had taken several teenagers in the last year and a half and five teens were still known to be missing. Needless to say, they told us that he was considered extremely dangerous. The man that John described fit the description of this serial killer and the police said that I was very fortunate to have averted a total abduction.

When I called home to talk to my parents, my mother said that she had heard about these abductions on the news and she wanted us to leave *British Columbia* as fast as possible. I agreed with her and we packed up our gear and left for *Alberta* right away. I was still shaken up by the whole event that occurred but felt very fortunate that John had come to my rescue. I kept thanking John for being so brave that night.

"My friend Jeremy who I saw earlier tonight had warned me about this *BC monster* that was on the loose in the area. When you wandered away, I wasn't taking any chances Jeanette," said John. "I followed you to make sure you would be safe."

"You're my hero John," I said. "Thanks again and you need to thank your friend Jeremy for warning you."

"I already did," said John.

That night, as we travelled back home on the road to safety, I broke down and cried. I realized then as I tried to clutch onto my sprit sand rock that it must have fallen off during the scuffle that I had with the *monster*. I also thought about how it had saved my life three times so far on this trip. I started to wonder though if this rock may have been bad luck instead of good luck all along. My bad luck hadn't started until after I found it. I realized though that it must have been good luck since it did help to save me from being shot by a hillbilly, from falling off a cliff and from being killed by the *BC monster*. I convinced myself to put all these silly *voodoo* thoughts out of my head and just felt happy that I was heading home.

Once we arrived back home in *London* several weeks later, Richard Reinhardt was sitting and talking with my mother on the front porch of our house as we drove up in the driveway. Richard got up out of his chair and waved to me. I looked at Maria and she asked me, "What is he doing here?"

"I don't know. I wonder how he knew we were coming home today," I said to Maria. All that went through my mind at this moment was how much I missed Eddie.

Richard said that he stopped by to see if we were home yet from our trip and asked my mother if she had heard from us. She said that she thought we would be home soon and also told him all about the brush that I had with the *BC monster*. He seemed to be genuinely concerned as he asked me, "Are you alright Jeanette? That sounds like it was a really scary situation to be in."

I told him that I was fine and went over to my mother and she gave me a big bear hug. My father then came out of the house also to welcome us back home.

We stayed up late that night telling them all the stories about the trip and how much of an adventure we had. I didn't say much about the attempted abduction just so that my parents wouldn't worry about the effects that the abduction had on me. I didn't want to dwell on the negative event of the trip but instead told them all about how I found *Canada* to be such a beautiful country with its diverse landscape. I also shuddered as I thought about the diverse people that I met on this trip. I was glad to have met the most handsome Eddie but was fearful about having met up with the ugly *BC monster*. It was an adventure that I would soon not forget.

CHAPTER NINE

Disappointment

Maria and I were both home the day that the phone rang and it was my mother's good friend, Martina Chavensky calling. She was the lady who had given both Maria and I the chance to work part-time on weekends at the deli-market that she owned in downtown *London*.

After my mother hung up the phone, I heard her say to my father, "She squeezes the blood from beneath my fingernails Peter. Someone took money from the till at the deli a couple of months ago. I can't take it anymore."

"Who took the money?" asked my mother when she came over to us and first looked at me. I had a perplexed look on my face and so she turned to Maria and asked,"How could you do that Maria? I hope you are satisfied now that both of you have been fired and I have lost a good friend. You're lucky she isn't going to press charges against you."

I suddenly felt sick to my stomach as I realized the reason why Maria always volunteered herself to close up the till at the end of our shift and directed me to do the dishes. I felt foolish as I had no idea that she was helping herself to the money. What made me feel worse was the thought that my mother's friend Martina probably thought that we both had stolen the money. A double trouble set of twins is probably what she thought. I now too was fired from the only job that I ever had, thanks to Maria's actions.

"This is the last straw Maria," yelled my father.

"I don't know where we went wrong," said my mother as she began to cry.

That's when the tempers flared between my father and sister and chairs were thrown. Literally, I witnessed in horror but didn't say anything as my father kicked Maria with his foot up the stairs and out of the house. I found out later that she left to go back to *Vancouver* with that loser boyfriend Larry who she met while bagging apples. I couldn't understand why Maria chose to leave with him but under the circumstances, I think she had no other choice but to leave and go back to a place that was somewhat familiar and far away. I hoped that she wouldn't be gone for long and that she would be back soon.

After Maria left, my mother cried a lot whenever I brought up the subject of how Maria might be doing out west and my father just grumbled and acted miserably. There was a very gloomy atmosphere that just hung in the house all the time. My parents acted like the world had ended without any hope for recovery.

"She'll be alright," I said to my mother as I tried to console her. Mom said, "As a mother you're only as happy as your unhappiest child." It seemed to weigh heaviest on my mother when there was no word from Maria.It's ironic how you find out later on in life that these sorts of moods tend to run in families. It seems clear to me now that Maria was a lot like my father with his moods that grabbed a hold of him from the moment the leaves fell off the trees in the fall until the first birds started to chirp in the spring. He was so moody during these times that he wouldn't talk to any of us for three weeks at a time. I knew to stay out of his way when he was like this from a young age. My oldest brother Matt also had little motivation at times in his life and instead of going to University as my parents had wanted him to; he chose to leave the house at age eighteen to work as far away from home as possible. He ended up going to work at a mundane job in *Alberta* during the *boom* years and did a lot of partying with his friends. From what I could see, Maria seemed to be inflicted with these same moods even to a greater extent than either my brother or father. If only Maria had received the help that she so desperately needed, things might have turned out differently for her.

After Maria got kicked out of the house, I felt lost without her around. I never did hear back from Eddie at all either. When I asked Mark how Eddie was doing out west, he simply told me not to take it personally but that he got back together with his fiancé after I left and they were getting married this Christmas. At this point, I felt upset about both my sister being gone and about Eddie not living up to the promise that he made to me. My self-confidence was already shattered after my encounter with the *BC monster* and now I felt that I needed a change in my life. That is how I ended up attaching myself to the first serious boyfriend that came along.

When I started University that fall, Richard needed a ride to school, so I picked him up along the way and ended up seeing him every day during the week. We also went out on the weekends with a group of friends and also played a lot of tennis, went skiing and sailed on his boat. I don't think I was ever really in love with him the way I was with Eddie though but Richard seemed to fill the void in my life at the time after my sister was gone. Then the day arrived not too long after when Richard told me that he loved me and it sounded like he meant it. Soon after when he asked me to marry him, of all things while I was peeling the potatoes, I accepted. He wasn't very romantic about it but at least we were engaged and I felt happy about starting a new life together.

"Let's have sex tonight Jeanette now that we are engaged," said Richard. "I've been waiting for this for a long time."

I was still a virgin and hesitated about sleeping with him before I was married but it all happened so fast that night and then as quickly as it started it was suddenly over. *Did I miss something?* I asked myself. *Why did I not feel happy about what just happened?*

I thought that the sex would improve between us once we were married but I never really enjoyed it with him and thought about other things while he did his business. There was no sexual spark between us, which was obvious in my mind. Whenever I brought up the subject of our sex life, Richard started to say something but then looked away and changed the subject. Whenever I talked about starting a family, he said that he wasn't ready. After several long years of catering to him, I felt it was time to do something to make myself happy in this dull marriage of mine. That's when I made the decision to unilaterally go off the pill and I became pregnant. Richard did not take the news well when I told him that I was going to have a baby.

"You can't be pregnant," stated Richard. "We can't afford to be."

Richard had been working at a car dealership as a salesman and sales had been slow that year because of the recession. I didn't care what he thought. I was looking for someone to truly love and the idea of this baby growing inside of me made me feel alive. Although my mother and father smiled at me when I told them that I was pregnant, I could see in my mother's face that she was not overjoyed with the news.

"Are you not happy for me Mom?" I asked her.

"Yes, I am excited with the news Jeanette," she said as she smiled at me. Then she quickly frowned and said very sadly, "I just can't help but think how Maria is doing out west. My biggest fear is that she has turned into a prostitute or is hanging out with a bike gang on the streets of downtown *Vancouver*."

I really didn't know what was going on with Maria either but I had the sense that she was alright. As her sister, I didn't worry about her well-being the way I saw that my parents did. It wasn't until years later when I had my own daughter that I realized the severity of the situation. Not knowing where your child was and having no contact with her what so ever must have been devastating for them. I only knew how it made me feel at the time. I felt really sad that Maria wasn't here to see my baby. That's when I decided to contact Maria through a mutual friend who knew where she was staying in *Vancouver*. I got Maria's phone number and called her to tell her my good news.

"You have to come home Maria," I pleaded with her. "You've been gone a long time."

"I'd like to but I'm not so sure I would be welcomed back home anymore," she said. "I think I'll move to *Ottawa* and stay with our cousin John for a while. That way, I'll be closer to home but not too close, if you know what I mean."

"Well, at least that is a little closer and you can come to London for visits," I said. "Mom and Dad will be happy to see you again."

"Like fuck," she said.

"I mean it Maria," I said. "They miss you and need you back in their lives. Mom has been having trouble with her back lately. She has been in a lot of pain. You need to come home."

For the time being, it seemed to me that everything was back on track. I was going to have a baby, my sister was back in my life and when I told my parents that Maria was coming back to live in *Ontario,* they showed enthusiasm about seeing her once again.

"I'll be happy to see Maria again even if it's just for five minutes," said my mother.

"As long as she can keep her hands in her pockets, I'll be happy," said my father.

"I'm glad that Maria will be moving to *Ottawa* and coming for a visit at Christmas time before you head down south for the winter," I said to both of them.

The visit with Maria was short and it left everyone satisfied to have seen one another again. Maria seemed to have matured a little since she came back from living out west and my parents acknowledged that. After Maria's visit, my parents travelled down south for the winter months and enjoyed camping in their trailer just like all the other *Canadian* snowbirds. Upon their arrival, my mother sent a postcard stating that they had arrived safely and that they would be back from their trip well before the baby was due to be born in a couple of months.

Within two weeks of their departure, my father called to say that they had arrived home early from their trip. My mother's back pain was increasingly getting worse and she couldn't sleep comfortably enough at night in the trailer so they had to come home. Up until then, she never had back pain in her life. Then the late night trips to the ER came when my mother told my father that she could not stand the pain any longer. Three different doctors sent her home on three separate occasions telling her to take *Tylenol* for what they thought was arthritic pain. Then after several long months of no real relief of the pain, my father told me that he was going to take my mother to a back clinic in *Toronto* to see if they could help her. I wanted to go with them but since my baby was due any time now, I couldn't go to lend my support. Instead I wished them luck as they wished me luck.

While I thought my mother was getting the relief she needed from her pain in a hospital in *Toronto*, I was having pain and giving birth to a son in a hospital in *London*. The pain that we both endured turned out to be from very different causes. At least I had the knowledge that my pain would soon give way to joy, not like my mother's pain that was constant and had become excruciating.

Before the baby was born, Richard and I had agreed that we would name the baby Peter Thomas after my father if it was a boy. Suddenly, after seeing the baby born Richard changed his mind and wanted to name him Nicholas Thomas after his own father instead. It really didn't matter to me at the time. *At least*, I thought, *he was finally taking an interest in this baby.* Richard smiled at me and looked so proud and happy so it seemed for the first time in a very long time. Once I arrived home from the hospital with my beautiful baby boy, my father called to tell me that he had returned from *Toronto* but that my mother was still in the hospital there. He went on to tell me that her back pain wasn't caused from arthritis at all. She had been diagnosed with pancreatic cancer that had invaded her body and she didn't have much time left to live.

How could this be? I asked myself. *Her birthday was next week and she was only turning sixty-seven years old and most importantly, she hadn't had the chance yet to hold my baby.* Being a new mother, it was an effort for me to bundle up my newborn and head all the way to *Toronto* to see her in the hospital but I felt that I had to go before it was too late. Even though she looked like she was in severe pain when I arrived, she gave me the biggest smile when she saw the baby and she got to hold her grandson for the first time. Little did I realize it at the time, it would also be the last time.

"Are you eating Mom?" I questioned as I noticed she looked so pale and thin.

"I tried to eat one lousy grape today but I couldn't. It just wouldn't go down," she said in a low voice as she turned away to look out the window. "Don't worry about me Jeanette. I have had my time and now it's your turn. Enjoy that beautiful baby for as long as possible before he grows up. It all happens so fast."

"I want you to enjoy him too Mom," I said to her as my eyes filled with tears.

"I will always be with you honey," she said. "Don't cry for me. I am going to a better place. The only rotten thing is leaving all of you behind. We will meet again, you'll see."

On her birthday, she was flown back to *London* by air ambulance. Some birthday present that turned out to be. It ended up that she was coming home so that she could see all of her children one last time.

When Maria and I arrived at the hospital in *London*, Mom was sleeping and her gown had come away from her shoulder and revealed how skinny she had become. All I could see was her skin over her bones that were sticking out. When she woke up as Maria and I approached the bed, I straightened out her gown and smiled at her.

As she tried to smile at us, she said, "Here are my darling twins, night and day different but forever best friends. Keep smiling you two. Life is too short to waste your time looking sad."

Mom was trying to give us some last minute advice before she was gone but I thought that she had instilled great values in all of her children and led the household well by her actions. It was up to each of us to listen to our conscience and make the right choices in life. Maria and I looked at each other as we left the hospital room that night and we both shook our heads. I knew then that it wouldn't be long. Within one week of her arrival back to *London* and once she had seen all of her children one last time, the time with her ended abruptly.

It was a very sad moment for me when I lost my mother. It was really so unexpected. It was like a slap in the face when I first heard that she had cancer and the doctors had predicted that she would only live between one to six months. I was really sad for my baby too who was only a week old at the time when she passed away. He would not get to know her at all as he grew up.

When I tried to discuss my loss with Richard, he shrugged his shoulders and told me that he had lost his own father to cancer when he was a teenager and there wasn't much you could do about it. There wasn't much consolation in his cold response. It was at that moment that I realized that life could be very disappointing, especially living it with a guy like Richard. *Why was he so cold?* I asked myself. *Was it too much to ask for a little compassion and support from him?*

CHAPTER TEN

The Betrayal

As he squeezed me tight and pulled me close, I could feel his cheek brush up against mine and as our lips met, we kissed passionately. As he caressed my body, it tingled all over. *Oh Eddie,* I thought.

Suddenly, a loud noise woke me up to reality and I found Richard snoring in bed beside me. I realized then that I had been dreaming about passion that was lacking in my life. Dreams usually have some hidden meaning and after several long years of marriage, any hint of romance had vanished and I longed for a loving intimate relationship. Then it occurred to me that Richard and I hadn't had sex for a while. I never referred to us as making love since it never felt that way. Suddenly, it alarmed me further to realize that my period had come and gone twice in that time and we had not had sex at all. I obviously wasn't missing it much but then I asked myself; *didn't the average married couple have sex at least once a week?*

When I confronted Richard with my observations, he just said that he had been too tired lately. It was true about him being tired. He was working long hours at the dealership and usually went out after work for a couple of beers with the guys to de-stress. Then the following Saturday night he said he was going out again with the guys but I protested and wanted him to stay home with me so that we could watch a movie. With a young baby in the house, we hadn't had a chance to have any fun together for quite some time and I thought it would be good for us to spend some quality time together. He said he had promised his buddy that he would go out to celebrate his birthday and he would only stay for a couple of beers. I wasn't happy with him choosing his friend instead of me but I thought that as long as he didn't stay out too late, we could still spend some time together when he got home.

After waiting up for Richard, I had fallen asleep on the couch and woke up when the phone rang at five o'clock in the morning. My heart was racing and I asked myself, *is Richard alright? Was he in a car accident?*

"Are you alright? Where have you been?" I asked him.

"Out driving around thinking," he said.

"You were out driving all night long? It's five o'clock in the morning!" I said as I focussed on my watch.

"Is it alright if I come home?" he asked.

I told him, "Of course you can come home. Why are you asking?"

At this point, I felt angry and confused and I didn't realize what was going on. When I think back to this time in my life, I feel embarrassed that I had no clue about the betrayal. As the saying goes, *the wife is the last to know.* Well, I was the last to know alright but it wasn't because he was good at deception. I trusted him blindly and I never would have thought that he was the type of guy to fool around. I thought that he was decent and it seemed like he came from a very good family and he loved me of course. *Why would anyone do that to someone that they loved?* I asked myself. You can tell my innocence or stupidity at the time, depending on how you perceive it.

When Richard came home, my radar was up though. I drilled him with questions and he seemed to have a plausible answer for each. Later that day, I found a pack of matches in his car from a motel in *St. Thomas* near where he worked and I immediately confronted him with that. He denied that the matches belonged to him. He told me that of course he didn't smoke but his buddy who he gave a ride home to that night did and he implied that he must have dropped it in his car. This sounded like a plausible answer that I believed to be true.

For the next couple of weeks, I looked for clues of any indiscretions but nothing materialized. I convinced myself that everything was alright between us. We had a few problems that we needed to iron out but nothing that I thought was too much to handle. All I thought was that maybe we needed to find a good babysitter so that Richard and I could go out for dinner and see a movie. We hadn't been out since Nick was born and it was now coming up to his first birthday. Up until now, I didn't trust just anyone to look after Nick. I didn't want to ask my father to babysit because he already looked after Nick during the day when I was at work and it really wasn't fair to ask him to babysit on the weekend as well. Richard's mother told me she couldn't babysit because she was afraid that she was too old to watch him so I had a bit of a dilemma.

After Nick's first birthday party, Richard told me that he needed time away to think about things and that he was going to stay at his mother's place for a while.

"You're leaving? Don't you love me anymore?" I asked. "What about your son?"

He shrugged his shoulders and said, "I'm sorry Jeanette but you always got more out of him than I ever did. I do hope you find someone one day who will appreciate you more than I ever could."

So off he went as I held Nick tight in my arms. *This couldn't be the end of us?* I asked myself. *He would be back after he figured things out but what was there to figure out?* He called me later that night to say that I didn't have to worry that he wouldn't fight for custody of Nick.

"What are you talking about and where are you?" I asked. In the background I could hear a child laughing. "What is going on? Who is that kid?" I asked. "Is there another woman?" I shouted. When he didn't answer me, I suddenly felt all the blood drain from my head down to my toes. I had finally put two and two together.

That night, Richard's mother called me up on the phone as well and started crying and said, "Not you two. It seems everyone is getting divorced these days. What will happen to poor little Nicholas without his parents together?"

"Well, why don't you ask your son that question," I said. "He's the one that walked out of Nicholas' life. Why don't you tell him yourself that what he has done is wrong?"

"I know he's at fault," she cried. "But I can't say anything to him. He's an adult now."

"Well," I said slowly. "You're right about one thing. He's an *adult*erer. Good-bye Janice. I don't feel like talking any further about this right now."

As I hung up the phone, I thought to myself that *the apple doesn't fall far from the tree.* I liked Janice but she wasn't being helpful to me right now. I missed my own mother more than ever right at this moment and I could have used her advice and support but I knew I had to stay strong for Nicholas.

Shortly after this time, Richard told me that he still wanted to be friends. *With friends like that, who needs enemies*, I thought to myself. It wasn't until much later that I learnt that he had many other women over the years while we were married. *Some husband he turned out to be*, I thought.

61

My thoughts now turned to Nicholas and I felt fortunate that I had him in my life. My biggest fear at the time was that Richard would change his mind and fight for custody of Nick but he gave up his parental rights and never seemed to even blink an eye over it. I just couldn't understand how he could just walk out of Nick's life so easily.

Good riddance, I thought. *I can do this on my own anyway.* I wasn't sure what the future held but anything was better than trying to mend a broken relationship with someone who was so deceitful. I called Maria to tell her about what Richard had done.

"I knew he was no good for you Jeanette," said Maria. "He's a very selfish type of guy. You're a strong person so I'm sure in time you'll be fine. At least you have Nick. He's the best part of the deal."

"I know that Maria," I said. "I just wish it didn't hurt so much. Dad is going to move in with me now that Richard is gone. At least I can feel good about him being here to look after Nick when I'm at work."

"That sounds like a good scenario for both of you," said Maria.

"Oh, I forgot to tell you the good news as well Maria. Nick took his first steps on his own today," I exclaimed. "Now I'll have to take my own first steps without Richard."

"You can do it," said Maria. "I have no doubt in my mind."

I was satisfied with the situation for now but as time moved on, deep inside I was longing for something more in my life and it seemed that paradise was just out of my grasp.

CHAPTER ELEVEN
To Love Again

Just as I was settling into a comfortable life with my son and adjusting to being a single mother, my father was diagnosed with prostate cancer and had to start injection treatments. He actually seemed happy with the diagnosis as he smiled while telling me about the news that he had received from the doctor.

"It's not that bad Jeanette," said my father rather matter of fact. "This is my ticket to see your mother again soon. If it wasn't for you and Nicholas in my life now, I would have wanted to go a lot sooner."

"I know your heart was broken after my Mom died and that you miss her so much Dad. Even though you live with us, I can tell you are lonely without her," I said.

"Don't worry about me Jeanette. You need to meet a good man that will take good care of you," he insisted.

I suddenly had to admit to myself that I was feeling somewhat lonely also. I was still only thirty years old and thought that maybe there was a man out there for me but I wasn't feeling overly confident about that at this time in my life.

My older cousin Melissa deValk was trying to convince me to get out of the house and to socialize and possibly meet a guy at the same time. She had been divorced for five years and was ready to meet the man of her dreams. I just wasn't very interested and I still didn't trust men so I convinced myself that I didn't need any man to make me happy. After Melissa kept after me to go out with her, I finally decided to go to the *Dutch-Canadian Club* on singles night with her thinking that it might be a good place to go and try to have some fun.

"What do you have to lose? It'll be good for you Jeanette. You'll see," she said positively.

It turned out to be a bit of a drag when I got there. Most of the people there were in their forties and the polka music they played was not my style. I left our table to go to the washroom and when I got back there was a guy sitting there with Melissa. She had invited him to sit with us when she saw that he was sitting all alone at another table.

"This is Douglas Bennett," she said. "What is it that you did for a living?"

"I'm a transport parcel logistics engineer," he said.

I laughed out loud while Melissa looked a little perplexed. He was a tall man with a muscular build and had an heir of confidence about himself when he spoke. He told us that he had come here to meet his friend Bruce Wade but that he was late and hadn't shown up yet.

"My buddy Bruce told me that I should go out and meet the girl of my dreams instead of sitting around being a miserable old fart all the time. I don't know where he is though. I guess he stood me up," said Doug.

"Well, I think you came to the right place though," said Melissa as she smiled at him.

"Do you like to polka?" asked Doug.

I just waved my hand and gestured no while my cousin jumped up and went out on the dance floor with him. As I watched them dancing, I thought to myself that it was nice to see Melissa having a good time. She had been mostly alone now that her children were teenagers and off doing their own thing and she seemed to be ready to have a new man in her life. When we left the club, my cousin said to me that she thought Doug was cute and that she really had a good time.

"He seems easy to talk to and at least you got me out of the house," I said. "You can have him though. I really don't have any interest in any guy right now."

"Okay," said Melissa as she smiled at me. "But I'm not desperate you know."

She seemed pleased that I had no real interest in Doug and confessed that she had given him her phone number so that she could get together soon with him to go dancing again. I thought that she was crazy to do so in this day and age.

"What if he is a serial killer like the *BC monster* that I encountered out west?" I asked. "You don't even know him," I warned.

"He seems like a nice guy to me and he's an engineer," she said.

"You're funny Melissa," I said. "He was just joking about being a transport parcel logistics engineer. He drives a transport truck and delivers freight. It's the same as a garbage man saying that he's a sanitation engineer. It's all to make the job sound better."

"Oh, now I get it!" she said. "I feel pretty dumb about that."

"And I thought I was slow when it came to understanding jokes!" I said to her. "It just goes to show you that you can't always believe what someone tells you without knowing all the facts. I think Doug seems to be a sincere guy though."

The following weekend, the phone rang and when I answered it, Doug was on the line and asked, "How are you doing Jeanette?" I was thrown off guard by his unexpected call and asked him, "How did you get my number?"

"Melissa gave it to me. I know the owner of a quaint restaurant and bar that plays better music than the *Dutch-Canadian Club*. Even though I like to polka, I'd rather dance to rock and roll," he said.

"You want to go on a real date?" I asked.

"Yes, a real date Jeanette. I'll pick you up on Saturday at six o'clock," he said without hesitation.

When Doug arrived to pick me up, he brought me some flowers. We left to go to the *Night Light* bar and grill in downtown *London*. The atmosphere was very romantic with soft music playing in the background when we walked in. We had an elegant candle light dinner with steak, mushrooms and a salad. After our dinner, the *DJ* picked up the pace of the music and started playing rock and roll and then the place came alive. We danced the whole night until one o'clock in the morning and at the end of the evening, Doug gave me a kiss that made my lips tingle.

"What was that for?" I asked.

He looked me straight in the eye and said, "That's thanks for the good time I had tonight and for you being you. It's been a long time since I met someone as nice as you."

When Doug dropped me off at home that night and went on his way, I felt exhilarated for the first time in a really long time. I thought about how he was so easy to talk to and how he listened with interest to all my stories about Nicholas. He said that we should go for a hike, all three of us to *Coldstream Conservation* area next weekend.

"What do you mean? Are you talking about going with you, me and Melissa?" I asked.

"No, No! You, me and Nicholas," he said.

On the following Saturday, we went for a long hike at the conservation area. I had brought a child carrying back pack to put Nicholas in and once he was in the back pack, we trudged through the snow along the trails. It was a picturesque park that had a fresh blanket of white powdered snow that had recently covered the entire ground. I was having such a good time until I put Nick in his car seat and we began to drive away. He started to cry and then he began screaming at the top of his lungs and I thought that there was seriously something wrong with him.

He must have a pinched nerve or he has a needle stuck in his side from his diaper, I thought to myself.

Nick wouldn't stop screaming and the tears were streaming down his face by this time. I pulled over to check on him and as I stopped the car so did Nick's screaming. There didn't seem to be anything wrong with him at all. He was having a temper tantrum and I didn't know why. I was so embarrassed by Nick's behaviour that I thought for sure this would scare Doug away for good.

"I'm sorry Doug," I said. "I'm not sure why he is having such a fit."

"I bet he just didn't want to leave the hike. Now he's my type of kid who enjoys the great outdoors," he said. "I'm sure you heard more whining from your ex-husband right?"

We both started to laugh and it felt good to laugh. It had been so long since I felt like laughing at all. I was glad that this little episode with Nick didn't scare Doug away. In fact, Doug started coming over to visit every weekend to spend as much time with Nick and me as possible. I enjoyed his visits and liked the fact that he always included Nicholas in our activities. We went for long walks and played with Nick at the park in my neighbourhood. Since I worked days and Doug worked nights, we made the most of the weekends that we had together.

It was during the week, while Doug was on his break in *Toronto* and while he waited for his truck to be reloaded that he gave me a quick call to see how things were going.

"How was your day Jeanette?" he asked.

"Not too bad," I said. "What about you?"

"I'm busier than a one-legged man in an ass-kicking contest. Not bad for an engineer that is," he answered.

"Oh Doug, you are such a clown," I said.

As our first Valentine's Day approached, Doug gave me a note on a small piece of paper that stated, *Dear Jeanette: Thanks for all the love that you and Nicholas have shown me since we first met. If this is a dream, don't wake me up. All my love forever, I hope, Doug.*

He also gave me a friendship ring and told me that he loved me. It scared me to think about that. I certainly wasn't ready to reciprocate with those words. Instead, I told Doug that maybe we should slow things down a little. In my mind, I needed a little more time to think about the direction that I thought our relationship was headed. The betrayal that I had from my first marriage was still freshly etched in my mind.

CHAPTER TWELVE

You Can't Hurry Love

Phil Collins said it best with his lyrics, *My Mama said, You can't hurry love, Oh you just have to wait, She said Love don't come easy, it's a game of give and take, you can't hurry love, Oh you just have to wait, trust in the good times no matter how long it takes . . .*

Well, *mama* was very wise as most mothers are. Love didn't come easy in my first marriage and even though I didn't try to hurry love along, I did have to wait a very long time before the good times did arrive. There did seem to be a game of give and take alright but I had to be the one to give and Richard was the one who would always take and after several long years with him, the wait was finally over. The good times didn't start until after I met Doug.

When I told Doug that I used to go camping with my family ever since I was a baby, he didn't seem to believe me that I actually enjoyed it. When I discussed going camping with him in the summer, it wasn't until I showed him pictures of my camping trips to *Barry's Bay, Tobermorry, Myrtle Breach* and all of the pictures of my trip out to the west coast that he slowly began to acknowledge that I might love to camp.

"I finally believe you Jeanette that you like to camp and that you are not just putting up a facade," said Doug. "My ex-wife Cheryl didn't like camping even though she told me that she did when I first met her. When she did come with me, she used to bring all of her make-up including her hair dryer to camp."

"What's the point of that?" I asked. "Who cares what you look like when you're camping?"

"You'd care if you looked like she did without all that make-up caked on," he said sarcastically. "She was so scary looking that she's the only person I know who has to dress down for Halloween."

"Richard never liked camping either. He said that he didn't like the sand that got caught between his toes. I think Richard and Cheryl would make a great couple," I said. "In fact, we should introduce them to each other."

"Yes, they could be called *Dumb and Dumber; Frick and Frack; Liar and Cheater* or *Shit and Syphilis*. What a perfect match they would be together," joked Doug.

We both laughed out loud and I thought that it was better to laugh about the past and to be free of all the misery and to finally enjoy the good times now that I had Doug. I even finally told Doug that I loved him and I meant it from the heart. He seemed pleased as he smiled at me and gave me a big bear hug.

The next day when Richard came by to pick up Nicholas for one of his visits that were few and far between, Doug happened to be there to open the front door. He smiled at Richard, stuck out his hand and said, "Hi Richard. I'm Doug Bennett. I wanted to personally thank you for screwing up your marriage. I'm very happy to have Jeanette."

As I peered from behind the door, I could see that Richard looked somewhat flabbergasted as he stood there with a blank look on his face. He didn't seem to know what to say in response to Doug's statement. Moments like that felt victorious even if it was at the expense of Richard's feelings but it was nothing compared to what he had put me through with all his lies and deceit. I knew all too well how it felt to be betrayed by the one you loved and thought you could trust.

Doug told me that he too knew how it felt to be betrayed by the one you loved. His best friend Darrell Mulligan had lost his job a few years ago and Doug was kind enough to invite him to stay at his house until he got back on his feet.

"What I didn't realize when I came home early from work one Friday night was that Cheryl and Darrell were doing the horizontal bop in my bed," said Doug. "I immediately told Darrell to get the fuck out of my house and I turned to Cheryl and told her that I now knew what she was all about and I didn't want anything more to do with her. I grabbed some of my personal belongings and left without ever looking back."

"That's terrible Doug to actually catch them in the act," I said.

"The gall of some people," he said to me. "She tried to apologize and then told me it was my fault for working nights and not being there for her. Can you believe that?"

"Yes, I can! Richard kind of said the same thing to me that he didn't think he was at fault for straying and that he barely cheated," I said in disgust.

"Isn't that like being only a little bit pregnant?" Doug asked. "He either cheated or he didn't. There's nothing in between in my opinion."

"I agree. He had no good reply because his actions didn't make good sense. I couldn't believe his nerve in just walking out, clearing out our joint bank account and forgetting about our son. He tried to say that he was sorry too, but the damage was done. Once a cheater always a cheater," I said.

"And he barely cheated, as if that made it all okay. I'm sure his ass was bare as he was cheating," said Doug as he laughed.

"It wasn't even about forgiveness. I could have probably forgiven him for what he had done to me but not for what he had done to our son. He didn't seem to care about him and that upset me the most. He walked out of his life and now he only picks Nick up for a visit when it is convenient for him," I went on to tell Doug.

"At least I never had any kids with Cheryl," Doug said. "It made the split a lot easier."

"I'm still upset with Richard from the last time that he was late for over half an hour before he called to cancel his visit once again," I said. "I had Nicholas all bundled up in his snowsuit and could see the disappointment on his face when his Dad didn't show up that night. I feel like kicking Richard in the groin the next time I see him but I guess he is Nick's father so he must have some rights."

"You should just kick him in the balls Jeanette. I'm sure you will get more satisfaction from that," said Doug. He pointed at the front door and said, "He gave up his rights the moment that he walked out that door and didn't care about Nick."

"I think he still does love Nick but in his own selfish way," I said. "I do know that Richard seems to be satisfied in knowing that I always take good care of Nick which means that he doesn't have to. I believe that every child needs a good father and that's where you fit in Doug. You'll have to be the father Nick wouldn't otherwise have in his life, if you are up for the challenge?"

"You bet honey," said Doug. "I'll be the best father I can be. Not like my old man."

Doug was estranged from his own father since the day that he turned sixteen. He told me that he would never treat his children the way that he was treated by his own father. He said he will just do the opposite of what his father had done. That meant listening and not yelling, going to school plays instead of going to the *Legion*, being involved with your children instead of being involved with the bottle and most of all it meant showing respect to the mother of your children by treating her with kindness instead of throwing punches at her.

"I had enough of my father's drunken behaviour the day I turned sixteen. He was drunk as usual and when he started swinging towards my mother, I popped him one right between the peepers," said Doug. "I told my mother that she should leave the bastard for good. I packed some of my clothes and left before he woke up from his drunken stupor."

"Some Sixteenth Birthday that was Doug," I said to him.

"Oh well, it was the best present I ever got, knowing that my mother finally had the courage to leave him and I felt better knowing that I stopped the abuse against her. It was a real struggle at first for me to support myself and go to school at the same time at that age but anything was better than living with that son-of-a-bitch," said Doug.

Doug had many stories to tell me about the abuse that occurred when he was younger.

"One day, when I was only eleven years old, my older brother decided to play a trick on me and thought it would be funny to disconnect one of the brakes on my bicycle. When I rode home I wasn't able to stop properly and ended up crashing into the garage and dented the wall. When my father saw what happened, he immediately grabbed me and started to beat me with a rod that he had sitting in the garage. I told him to stop but he just beat me harder. Luckily, I was wiry at that age and was able to wiggle out of his grasp and run away before he beat me up too badly," said Doug.

"That's horrible," I said as I cupped my mouth. "That's child abuse!" I exclaimed. "Where was your mother at the time when this happened?"

"She was working," he said.

"Did she know about the abuse?" I asked sullenly thinking that if she had known about what was going on that she surely would have protected him.

"She knew. Her hands were tied. She wasn't able to stand up to him because that would mean she would get a worse beating herself," he explained.

"That's not right Doug. By not protecting you from him, she enabled him to continue the abuse. Besides, she should have called the police," I said.

"She was too afraid of what he would do to her if she did that," said Doug. "That wasn't the worst thing that ever happened. One night, my Dad had some buddies over and got stinking drunk as usual. Mom was in her bedroom hiding out of his way and I was out of the house as usual. I didn't ever dare to be home at night and certainly made sure that I never brought any of my friends home to see the drunken fest. When I finally did get home later that night, I saw the light on in my Mom and Dad's bedroom. I heard some noise coming from their room and then heard my Dad say to this guy Roy that it was his turn now. I was horrified to see all these grown men waiting in line for their turn with my mother in the bedroom."

"Oh Doug," I cried. "What happened next?" I asked.

"I ran down the laneway and out to the next farm house as fast as I could. I knocked on the door of my neighbour and asked if I could use his phone. Mr. Lewis took one look at me and asked if everything was alright. I told him I needed to call my uncle to come over since my Dad had hurt himself. He wanted to come over to help but I told him that it wasn't necessary."

"Did he believe you Doug?" I asked.

"Not really. I don't think so but I insisted that I wanted to call my Uncle Joe to come over. He only lived five minutes away. When he showed up he grabbed each of those drunken guys by the scruff of their necks and easily shoved them in the back of his pick-up truck. He told my Dad that if he ever caught him being this stupid again that he would call the police."

"That's a really shocking story Doug," I said. "How could he do that to your mother?"

"I don't know how he could do that Jeanette but it wasn't too long after that, when I ended the reign of terror by punching his lights out and I left for good. My Mom also had enough after that incident and she finally had the courage to leave shortly after."

At this point, I thought about my own childhood growing up and how happy it had been in comparison to Doug's childhood. I couldn't imagine living in a house full of so much abuse. I thought about the fact that everyone has only one childhood to live and I felt terrible for Doug that he was robbed of it and there was no turning back the pages to make up for it.

Now my own father's life was coming to an end and he spent his last days in *Parkwood Hospital* where I was happy that he got the best of care. I went to visit him everyday and when I brought Nicholas with me, his whole face lit up. He seemed happy to see us but asked, "Where's Maria?"

I had to think quickly and make up some excuse why she couldn't be there. He told me that he had made up his mind not to include Maria or Matt in his *Last Will and Testament* for any inheritance.

"They never come to see me, so they don't deserve any money," he said rather coldly.

"You don't really mean that do you Dad?" I asked. "What about Mom? She wouldn't be happy with that decision at all. She always treated all of her children the same."

"Well, she's not here now is she," he said. "I'll have to think about it. I have nothing better to do right now anyway."

As I wheeled my father around the hospital grounds and as we talked about how Nicholas was growing up to be a sweet little boy, he seemed to be in a happy mood. We talked a great deal too about his life that he had spent with my mother and how glad he was to have met and married her.

"Dad, why didn't you ever try to meet anyone else after Mom passed away?" I asked him. "Even just for companionship?"

"Once I had the best, the hell with the rest," he replied.

"You look great today Dad," I said as I smiled at him.

"Don't shit me little one," he said. "It's just the glow before the end. Thanks for everything you've done for me Jeanette."

I was awake at one thirty in the morning when the call came from the hospital that my father had passed away. As soon as the phone rang, I jumped out of bed and I knew who it was. The nurse said her condolences to me and then told me that my father had gone peacefully in his sleep. She also told me that I could wait until the morning to gather up his belongings.

My father had made me executor of his *Last Will and Testament* so that meant that I had to take care of the usual arrangements for the funeral and splitting out of his estate. When I opened up his *Will*, I looked at what he had written in it. *I bequeath all my estate and belongings to be split out between my three children, Mark Peter Vandermeer, Jeanette Marie Vandermeer and Ronald Michael Vandermeer. I also give my Honda Civic car to Jeanette Marie Vandermeer as special thanks for taking great care of me while I was sick.*

I thought to myself, *What about his other two children?* On the next page, he had scribbled at the very end of the *Will*, *I hereby leave ten thousand dollars each to my other two children, Matthew William Vandermeer and Maria Juliana Vandermeer. Your mother in heaven made me give you something. You're lucky that you get anything at all, Dad.*

When I distributed the money to each of my brothers and to Maria, I did not mention what my father had stated in his *Will* but gave each their share of the estate. The comments I received were varied. Both Mark and Ronald accepted the money and thanked me for taking care of Dad while he was sick over the last few years. When I handed Matt his share of the inheritance he asked, "Is that it? Where's the rest?"

As I handed Maria her cheque for ten thousand dollars, she stated, "That's not enough."

They both looked discontented with their share of the inheritance and it was only at that very moment that I understood why my father had done what he did.

CHAPTER THIRTEEN

The Fun Years

When Doug asked me to marry him, it wasn't while I was peeling the potatoes. He had surprised me one night while we were out dancing. My favourite song was playing that night, *Two Hearts* by *Phil Collins*. He asked me to dance and as he got me out on the dance floor, he kept smiling at me. Then as the song ended, the spot light came on and in front of all these people; he pulled out a ring and said to me, "Jeanette, I love you." Then he asked, "Will you marry me?"

"Yes, I will," I said excitedly. I knew that I was not just in love with Doug but that we had formed a family already that included Nicholas. We kept the wedding small with close family members and good friends attending. We ended up having our reception at that quaint little restaurant where we had our first date. There was plenty of good food and dancing to good music.

Doug and I kept smiling at each other and I felt so naturally happy that day. When Doug called me on the phone before the ceremony that day, he said that at his first wedding, he had woken up in the morning with a massive migraine headache. His best man at the time had warned him that it was a bad omen and told him that he didn't have to go through with it if he didn't want to.

"Today is so different Jeanette. No migraine," Doug went on to tell me. "We are two hearts that can now beat as one." He could be so romantic and I wallowed in it. It felt refreshing not only to give love but to receive it back in return.

At the wedding reception, my oldest brother Matt, who had returned from out west and had become a smooth-talking salesman, was there to make a heart-felt but quirky toast.

"Here's to the happy couple, Jeanette and Doug Bennett. May you keep your love alive as I'm sure you will and keep smiling you two. Jeanette, I love you and I know you made the right choice this time. Doug, glad you are part of the family now. You're the right man for the job."

My brother was right when he stated that Doug was the right man for me but I didn't like the fact that he inferred that being married to me was work. Doug laughed and said, "Thanks Matt but that's one job I know is the best job in the whole world. I couldn't be a happier man right now."

I felt flattered and liked how Doug turned it around and made me feel special.

We left for our honeymoon the next day and went to *Toronto Island*. We toured around the island on our bicycles and enjoyed the trails that meandered all over the island. I had a child seat on my bicycle for Nick so that he was able to come with us and enjoy the great view of *Lake Ontario* surrounding the island. We took Nicholas to an amusement park and took turns taking him on all the rides. It was a lot of fun to have Nicholas come with us on our honeymoon and it was a great feeling that Doug agreed that we were not going to leave without Nicholas. I loved the fact that Doug always treated Nick as his own son and this gave me the satisfaction of knowing that he would be there for Nick when he needed him the most.

Nine months later came our baby, Peter Thomas. He was named after my father and he was born on Valentine's Day.

"He's our love child," I said to Doug. "The best Valentine's gift I ever had."

"Conceived on that wild wedding night on *Toronto Island*," Doug said. "We were humming that night, baby!" Doug exclaimed. I thought back to that night when we woke Nick up in the middle of the night with our passionate cries.

"Are you okay Mommy?" Nick asked innocently.

"Yes, Yes Nick, I'm fine. Sorry to wake you. Please go back to sleep," I said.

Now, I finally understood what my *Tante* Wilma had said to me all those years back that, "Love can be complicated, but if you simply respect each other and have open communication and great sex, you will do fine." Doug and I certainly had a lot of respect for each other and always had good communication and great sex too. I realized that sex was not dirty and out of respect for each other and through good communication, the love flowed.

Richard had wanted me to always get in the mood by watching pornographic movies with him but I found them to be vulgar. He also used to go to the strip bars and tell me that he liked to get his appetitive wet so that he could come home for a meal. I felt just like a piece of meat when he would say things like that to me.

It wasn't until I met Doug that I felt the love that flowed between us. From that first kiss that he gave me that made my lips tingle on our first date, to the love making we have now, it was like paradise.

On our honeymoon, Doug said to me, "I really like all the loving, touching and squeezing that we have together. Do you remember that night early on when we first met, when I tried to put the moves on you baby? You looked embarrassed and told me you were not ready. Well, that was a test."

"That wasn't very nice of you Doug!" I exclaimed. "At the time, I was struggling with the thought of whether or not to sleep with you. I liked you a lot but knew it was too early in our relationship for that. What if I had said yes?"

"Then, we wouldn't be here right now talking to each other that is for sure," he said.

"I was glad that after I said no to you, that you didn't press the issue," I said. "I respected that. You don't know how happy I am that you don't have to get your jollies from all that dirty crap."

"I don't need that shit to make me happy. Just you," he replied as he gave me a gentle kiss. "Guys from work have called me queer when I wouldn't go out with them after work to the strip bars. I think it's degrading to the human body."

"I never understood how guys get their thrills through all that debauchery," I said. "I'm glad I have you Doug."

I was so happy when Peter arrived so that there was a brother for Nicholas. Nick seemed to adore his little brother and called him the *Snork* since he made funny sounds when he laughed. Peter's laugh was hysterical, the kind of belly-aching laugh that was very catchy.

After Peter was born, I asked Doug what he thought of going to visit his own father. Up to now, he had not bothered and they hadn't spoken to each other in over sixteen years.

"There's nothing like a new baby to break the ice and make a fresh start," I suggested.

"Well, I heard from my brother that my Dad had quit drinking so I guess it might be worth a try," he replied.

During our visit, Doug's father seemed genuinely thrilled to see his grandson for the first time as he held him tight and smiled at him. He later confessed to us, "Booze can destroy a family. Looks like you have a great family here. Keep it that way."

When we arrived back home from the visit, Doug asked me, "Can you believe that he said that Jeanette, that booze can destroy a family? This came from a man that used to get so drunk that I would have to pick him up from the *Legion* even though I was too young to drive. I had to make sure that he got home safely and didn't drive home drunk and kill some innocent person along the way."

"People can change over time and I feel that he is trying to put his best foot forward now. I think that it must be his way of apologizing to you for the hurt that he caused many years ago," I replied. "I'm glad for you that you have a chance to rekindle a relationship with him now that he's off the booze."

That night I knew the scars from Doug's past were deep when I saw him sitting up at the end of our bed and heard him crying softly in the middle of the night. He told me that he had these recurring nightmares from the past that haunted him. The flashbacks were so real and vivid in every detail that it felt as if it all happened yesterday.

"I didn't mean to wake you up dear. I'll be alright, go back to sleep," he said softly.

"You should get these feelings out," I replied.

By seeing his father that day, he had not only rekindled a relationship with his father but it had also rekindled the nightmares. We ended up staying up for the rest of the night and we talked and hugged and cried together. Doug said he had never told anyone about what happened in those dark years from age eleven to sixteen and it felt good to get it all out.

Twenty months after Peter came another baby. When I was in labour the doctor asked me, "Are you ready to have this baby?"

"Do I have a choice in the matter?" I asked as the labour pains were getting more intense.

"No, here comes the head. Push. Here are the shoulders, push!" ordered the doctor.

All I could think of at that moment was, "*Here comes another boy and I'll have three sons.*"

"Must be another boy with shoulders like that!" commented Doug as the baby started to arrive.

"Now wait a minute. We have to wait until the rest comes out. Push again," cried the doctor. Out came the baby and he commented, "Well, it's a girl."

"It's a what?" I asked as I gazed at my beautiful daughter.

"It's a girl! We can name her after your mother, Jennifer Marie," said Doug. "She looks perfect to me."

I was so surprised to have a little girl arrive after having convinced myself that I was carrying another boy. In my excitement, I asked the doctor if after delivering thousands of babies in his lifetime, if it felt like it's just another baby to him.

He replied, "Never. It's a miracle every time. She looks like a keeper to me."

Our family was now complete and in the meantime, Maria had returned to *London* after living for several years in *Ottawa*. I was happy that she had decided to come back to live in *London* after she met and married Andrew Orr and had two children in between the times that I had Peter and Jennifer. Seth and Emily were cute little kids but they were very busy children who never seemed to be able to sit still.

Whenever we got together with Maria and Andrew, it became apparent that something was wrong. Our visits were always cut short when Andrew started to drink. He wouldn't stop until he passed out cold from drinking all the beer that was in his fridge. When I asked Maria what was going on, she told me that Andrew was, "Fucked up."

"His headaches are getting worse as well," said Maria.

"Has he been to the doctor?" I asked Maria.

"Yes, the doctor told him that he has cluster headaches and by drinking, it only makes it worse," said Maria. "There's no pain medication that can dull this type of pain. He just got fired from his job because of these headaches interfering with his abilities to do his job. He seems really depressed right now."

"That's really awful to hear," I said to Maria.

Later when I told Doug about Andrew's headaches he only said, "Andrew doesn't have both oars in the water. He should give his hat another half-turn since it's not on tight enough."

"I know you don't like drunks Doug but I think he's been drinking to literally try to drown his pain," I said.

"I don't care what his reason is," said Doug. "I don't feel sorry for him and now he's lost his job because of booze and he has two small children to support. What about them?"

Later that evening, the phone rang and it was Maria on the line. It was difficult to understand what she was saying at first. She was crying and trying to tell me something about Andrew being gone.

"Gone, gone where?" I asked.

"He's gone! He fucking gassed himself in the car last night," she cried.

"You're kidding me right?" I questioned her in disbelief.

"No. He's gone. He only left a note by the laundry that stated, *Maria, there's a life insurance policy at my work. It's not much but it's all I have to offer, Andrew.*

Wow, what a waste of a life, I thought to myself. Suicide was such a final solution to what should only be a temporary problem. It was a last desperate effort to stop a pain where there's no hope left. I guess Andrew thought the world was better off without him. I didn't realize it at the time and although it sounds cruel to say, perhaps he was right for the first and last time in his life.

Just when life was the happiest for our family after little Jennifer was born, this tragedy occurred to knock the fun out of life for a while and to bring me down to reality. Maria's mood took a drastic turn downward at this point and she slipped into a depressive state. She didn't leave her house and she stopped coming over for visits. I felt a great sadness for Maria and her children and knew that she needed me more than ever now but as she had her challenge in life, I was about to have mine as well.

CHAPTER FOURTEEN

Tragedy

The unthinkable happened one early evening in late fall after Andrew had committed suicide. After the tragedy from this senseless act, I wasn't prepared for what else was to happen next in life. As I went into the kitchen, my eye caught sight of flames out of the window shooting up from the back deck of our house. I tried not to panic and felt my heart start to pound. I yelled out, "The house is on fire!"

The kids jumped up and I told them to get out of the house through the front door and wait in the spot where we had talked about when we had practiced our fire drills. They surprisingly remained calm and Peter grabbed his guinea pig and told Jennie to find the cat and take them outside. Meanwhile, Doug went running outside with Nicholas to investigate the fire. The flames were shooting twenty feet high engulfing the top of the roof. I immediately grabbed the phone and called *911*. The fire trucks came blaring to the house within two minutes and the firemen swiftly burst through the garage with their fire hose and put the fire out in seconds.

The fire chief asked if anyone was left in the house and if we were okay. I replied that we were a little shaken up and that we were all out of the house. When he saw where the kids had gathered, he told them that he thought they did a great job of getting out of the house, grabbing their pets and going to a safe designated place and remaining calm until help arrived.

It seems we were lucky to have averted what could nearly have been a tragedy. Little did I know at the time that this near tragedy was nothing compared to what happened to our neighbour down the road that night as well.

I apologized to the fire chief for calling him since Doug had almost had the flames out with the garden hose before the firemen arrived. He said to me, "Never apologize for calling *911*. You made the right decision to call as soon as you saw those flames. Never hesitate to call because seconds count when you are talking about a fire. Even though your husband seemed to have things under control, fire is unpredictable and could start up again if it isn't completely put out."

The damage to the house was minimal except for the deck where the flames had started. Later on that evening, I said to Doug, "We were lucky tonight that worse things did not happen from that fire. I can't imagine what could have happened had we been asleep when the fire broke out and it could have spread throughout the house."

"I almost killed us all tonight Jeanette," said Doug as he bent his head down. "I'm really sorry."

I could see that Doug looked upset about what happened that night. It was his mistake that had started the fire. He had emptied out the ashes from the fire place the day before and had left them in a bag on the wood deck at the back of the house like he always did without incident. The fire chief had explained that sometimes ashes may seem to be out but embers can smoulder for days and then ignite.

"Not to worry Dougie," I said. "It was an honest mistake. We all make them."

Then we heard about the real tragedy that occurred that night to one of our neighbours and how the unthinkable can happen when you least expect it. Our neighbour from across the street dropped by to make sure that everything was alright after seeing the big red fire trucks come wailing into the neighbourhood.

"Glad everything's okay with all of you," said Janet Rae. "Did you hear what happened to little Megan Walker down the street?"

"No, we were a little preoccupied tonight. What happened?" I asked.

"She went to the hospital with stomach pains last night but she's not coming home," said Janet sadly.

"What do you mean, she's not coming home?" I asked in shock.

Janet went on to tell us how little Megan was having such severe pains in her abdomen that her parents took her to the Emergency. She had appendicitis and her appendix burst while she was in the hospital. The doctors had to operate right away and it ended up that she died from sepsis which is a blood infection caused from all the toxins that were released after the appendix had burst.

"Wow," I said to Janet. "Our near tragedy is nothing compared to that tragedy. I still can't believe that she is gone."

I thought about Megan and how she was a sweet little girl with blonde hair and beautiful green eyes. She was full of life and was always smiling. She never walked anywhere but ran and said, "Ta-da here I am!" She had so much energy and spunk and all that came to an abrupt end at the age of eight. What happened that night to Megan was every parent's worst nightmare.

There were hundreds of people who gathered for the funeral three days later. There were family members, friends, hockey team mates, teachers and neighbours who attended. When we arrived at the funeral home, I could see the open casket from a distance. It all seemed so surreal and as I approached the casket, I could see her tiny figure as she lay there lifeless. It was so crowded in the funeral home with so many people wanting to say good-bye to Megan that we had to stand at the rear of the funeral parlor for the whole procession.

Megan's brother, Cory Walker, who was only ten years old, was nicely dressed in a black suit and tie and stood at the pulpit in front of the crowd of people. Everyone fell silent as he spoke first and directed his words towards his little sister laying there in the coffin.

"Megan you were not just my little sister, you were my friend. I will miss you forever. I know you must be a true angel because you have gone to heaven where only angels live," said Cory.

Then Megan's oldest brother, Stephen Walker, who was twelve and all dressed up as well, spoke next. "Megan you are so sweet. I liked it that you always liked doing boy stuff like playing soccer, hockey and going fishing. Remember the time we all went to the cottage in *Sturgeon Bay* and you caught the biggest fish. We wanted to help you reel it in but you wanted to do it all by yourself. You fought with that fish until you landed the big one. I'll never forget you little munch kin."

Megan's mother spoke next. "Sweetheart, you have been a blessing to this family. We are so lucky to have had you in our lives even if it was just for a short time. You've touched the hearts of so many here on earth and now it's time to touch the hearts of all those in heaven. We'll miss you forever."

Last but not least, Megan's father spoke. "Megan sweetie, our lives here will never be the same without you. Our hearts ache as we say good-bye to you today. We know we shall meet again one day. In the meantime, we will miss your dynamite smile, your grizzly bear hugs and your slap shot too. We love you Megan."

After the family spoke, you could feel the sadness permeate throughout the room. Most of the families who had gathered here had children who were around Megan's age and I realized that the tragedy that befell this family could have been dealt upon any one of us. When a tragedy like this strike, it seems that you find yourself asking, *why do things like this have to happen?* No matter what the answer is, it never seems satisfactory.

Looking around, I noticed that my neighbour, Shawn Stevens, who had only one child, a daughter the same age as Megan, broke down hysterically as he sobbed into his hands. I was all choked up thinking how awful this must be for this family to lose their little angel. It would be a long time before this family would gain any sense of recovery. At the end of the funeral everyone was given a pink balloon filled with helium and asked to gather outside the building in the parking lot.

As we all gathered outside, Megan's family each held a pink balloon in their hands as well. They looked up at the sky and asked everyone to repeat after them, "This is for you Megan, Ta-Da!" They then let their balloons go and everyone watched them float up and away. Then the family gestured to everyone else to do the same. One after another, people let go of the balloons and shouted, "This is for you Megan, Ta-Da!" It was amazing to hear hundreds of people repeat that phrase and watch all those balloons going up to heaven.

CHAPTER FIFTEEN

Nick

When Nick entered high school, I started to see signs of trouble. Out of the blue, he took my credit card and ordered an on-line adventure game, without my consent. When Doug and I confronted him, he said that he was sorry but he just had to have that game to play. He sounded very obsessed about it.

Then trouble started at school as well and his grades started to slip. He had always been a co-operative student with a steady *B+* average. He was likeable among his classmates and teachers and never caused any real difficulties. He was a responsible teenager who looked after his younger brother and sister after school while I was at work.

Then one day I got a call at work from Peter telling me that he and Jennifer had locked themselves in the bathroom upstairs because Nick was after them with a knife. He told me that they managed to grab the cat, some crackers and the phone and locked themselves in the only room in the house where they felt safe. I wasn't sure what to think. It all sounded a little bizarre to me.

"That's not funny Peter," I told him. "What's really going on? Let me speak to Jennifer."

When she came on the line she blurted out that Nick was crazy and he had a knife and was chasing them with it and she began to cry. I told her to hang on tight and I would be home right away. Once I got home, everything seemed fine. Nick said he was sorry and was only joking and tried to scare them for fun. I told him that I would see what Doug had to say about all this and that he would be punished. I couldn't tolerate that kind of behaviour.

Although Nick seemed to be better for a while, he increasingly seemed irritable and constantly fought with his brother and sister to the point that they both said that they hated him.

"I wish he was dead," said Peter.

"Now, that's not a very nice thing to say about your brother," I said.

"I don't care, I hate him and he's not my real brother anyway. He's only a half-brother," wailed Peter.

"That's a strong word *hate*. I hope you don't really mean that Peter. Don't ever say you hate someone," I said.

"Okay, I dislike Nick and I wish he was dead," yelled Peter.

It bothered me to hear that the children were not getting along very well. I had to admit to myself that Nick had been acting very peculiar lately by following me around the house and sticking to me like glue. He seemed a bit lost and when he spoke he talked so quickly that it was hard to follow what he was saying. It was getting a lot harder to get him up out of bed in the morning to go to school and he seemed to be down about something. When I confronted him and asked him what was wrong, he never seemed to know what was really bothering him. I tried to reassure him that everything was going to be fine but that he needed to be more respectful to his brother and sister.

He agreed that he was going to try harder and he asked if he could have some of his friends over on the weekend. I agreed and everything was fine until I came down and found them all gawking at a dirty magazine. They all laughed when I asked who brought the magazine over to my house. My heart sank when they all pointed at Nick.

I was angry with Nick and told him that he was grounded. He confessed that he had taken the magazine from his father's house and didn't think it was a big deal. He grabbed for his head and said he was sorry. I told him that I was really disappointed in his behaviour and I wasn't going to put up with it.

For weeks after, he became more distraught and didn't say or do much of anything. He lost interest in his computer games and listening to music and hanging out with his friends. I was worried about him and wondered if this was all just normal teenage behaviour. I kept telling myself that he was just going through a phase and that everything was going to be fine. Doug and I discussed our worries and he too said that he was becoming concerned.

The worst night came when Nick met me at the door when I came home from work and held his finger up to his lips and said, "Shish Mom. They'll hear you. Come on inside, quick."

"What are you talking about Nick?" I asked.

"They're after me Mom. I saw the delivery guy with his scanner across the street from our house. He is looking for me," he said. He looked terrified. "I heard the helicopters too Mom. They're going to take me away."

I honestly did not know what was going on. I called Doug and said he needed to come home right away. I told him that Nick was really upset and talking nonsense.

When Doug came home, all I could say to him was, "Nick is fucked in the head." I never swore unless I was really upset so Doug could tell that I wasn't kidding around. When I explained all that was happening with Nick, he decided to call the children's help phone and find out what we should do. I was glad that he took the initiative to call because I was too upset to think straight. What they told him was that it sounded like Nick needed some help and that he should be taken to the closest Emergency Paediatric hospital and if he refused to go, to call the police to give him an escort.

"A police escort?" I asked Doug. "He's not a criminal. What are they talking about?"

Doug said they told him in no uncertain terms that he should bring him to the hospital without delay and if he refused to go, we should call *911*. Doug started to dial *911* and Nick told him to stop and he reluctantly agreed to go with me.

It was a long drive to the hospital and Nick didn't say much. He held his head in his hands and muttered that he wanted the voices to stop. My heart sank when he told me this. I tried to reassure him that I was going to get him the help he needed. I could tell he was scared and I kept reassuring him that we were in this together and he didn't have to go through this alone.

When we arrived in the triage section of the hospital, the nurse asked me why we were here and I didn't know what else to say other than, "My son is depressed." She looked at Nick and quickly took us to a quiet room down the hall where we could wait until another nurse could assess our situation. I was grateful for the seclusion so that I could gather my thoughts.

The nurse that came into the room started gathering the normal information of name, age, family doctor's name, history of illnesses and ailments. Once she completed asking the easy questions, she then asked, "Now you say your son is depressed? Did he recently break up with his girlfriend? A lot of teenagers come in here with what they call depression because their girlfriend or boyfriend broke up with them and they can't live without them."

"No, he doesn't even have a girlfriend. He's been hearing voices and he can't sleep. His appetite has been down and he seems paranoid," I said. It was difficult to talk about what had been going on with Nick when I didn't even fully comprehend it all myself.

"Oh," she said. "We'll have to page the resident psychiatrist but before we do, we have to make sure there is a real need to do so."

I thanked her and wanted to cry but I told myself I had to keep strong for Nick. He was confused and scared and asked when we were going home. It was a long two hour wait before the doctor came in. He told us his name was Dr. Chan and asked how he could help us. I went over all the problems that we had been having with Nick lately including the knife incident, the paranoia and the voices he was hearing. He was sympathetic and had a soothing voice when he spoke, "It sounds as if Nick has some issues."

Then he turned to Nick and asked him if he took any drugs. He reassured him that he wouldn't be in any trouble if he had done a little experimenting and that it was really important to tell us if he was.

"We can test you to see if there are any drugs in your system so to save us all valuable time, we need you to tell us the truth Nick," said the doctor.

Nick just hung onto his head and looked like he was about to burst out crying. I interjected, "He doesn't do any drugs. What can you do to help?"

"Well," he said. "I'm only the resident psychiatrist on staff tonight. I'll have to call the head psychiatrist and see what he suggests. I'm sorry, I know it's late in the evening but we will do everything in our power to help your son as best as we can."

By now, all I could think of was that Doug was at home with the other kids and would be worried and wondering what was happening here at the hospital. I knew I couldn't leave Nick alone to make a phone call so I told the nurse that we were just going down to the pay phones to call my husband and that we would be right back.

"Oh Doug, it's been gruelling but I don't know how much longer we'll be here. I love you," I said.

He said, "I love you too honey. Please don't you worry about all of this, everything will turn out alright. I promise you. Be strong," he said.

It felt good to hear his voice and be reassured that I had the support of my husband. *Where was Nick's real father while all this was happening?* I questioned myself. He was nowhere in sight. He couldn't handle any crisis and it was better that he wasn't here to complicate matters. I did wish that Doug could have been with me at the hospital because he was always very much in tune with Nick and observed things that I didn't always notice.

After another two hours, the resident doctor came back in the room to ask how things were going. He advised us that after he spoke with the head psychiatrist, there was no debate whether or not Nick needed help but there was the question of whether it would be as an inpatient or outpatient of the Child and Adolescent ward. They finally agreed that it would be best for Nick to be admitted that evening so he wouldn't be a threat to himself or anyone else but they had to make sure that a bed in the ward was available. I felt both relieved that Nick would get the help that he needed but saddened that I would have to leave him in the hospital.

We made the trek to Nick's room and I had to convince him to be brave and that I would be back first thing in the morning to see him. He cried and told me he didn't want me to go. I told him that I loved him and to remember what I told him earlier about not having to go through this alone but that I had to go for now. It was a long and painful drive back home that night.

The next day Doug and I dropped off Peter and Jennifer at Maria's house so that we could go visit Nick in the hospital and talk to all the doctors. The nurse had told me the night before not to come in to see Nick too early because they were going to give him some medication to help him sleep. He was exhausted and needed a good night's sleep which would help him with his thoughts.

When we arrived, I remember thinking how horrible it would be to be left in this sterile environment in the state of mind that Nick was in and I wasn`t prepared for what was to follow. There was question after question and analysis of our lives and the lives of our extended family members on both sides.

"Is there mental illness in the family?" asked one of the doctors.

"No," I said.

"What about on your side Doug?" asked another doctor.

"Some are a little *Cuckoo* depending who you ask but Nick is my step son. I've known him since he was one and a half," said Doug.

"Well what about on Nick's biological father's side?" asked the first doctor.

I had to shove Doug under the table with my leg because I knew that he wanted to say something like, *now that's a loaded question, didn't you know he's the poster child for Psycho Boy?* This was not the time for making jokes.

"I'm not sure to tell you the truth," I said. "Nick's father hasn't been a big part of his life and I only knew his sister and mother who seemed fine to me. Nick's father does suffer from depression though."

"Was he or anyone else on his side of the family, mother, father, brother or sister ever on any medication for depression or was he or anyone else ever hospitalized for a mental illness?" said the second doctor.

"No," I said. "Again, I don't know that much about his side of the family."

"What about Schizophrenia?" asked the second doctor. "It usually strikes in the later teen years and Nick is only twelve. Sometimes traumatic events in a person's life can trigger this type of illness at a younger age. Events such as losing a parent or being the victim of abuse or witnessing a horrific accident can trigger this disease earlier in someone who is pre-disposed."

I answered simply, "Nothing like that has happened to Nick other than my father passed away from cancer a few years ago and he and Nick were very close. I know Nick misses him very much."

"I don't think that has triggered his mental illness. When I spoke with Nick, he confessed that he wanted the voices to stop. He couldn't think straight and he couldn't sleep for fear they would get him. There's no doubt in my mind that he is in a paranoid state but it's these voices that he's hearing that are most concerning," said the first doctor.

"What does all this mean and what happens now?" I asked.

"Well, usually mental illness runs in families. It's genetic. The best course of action is to start him on anti-psychotic medication for his paranoia and give him an anti-depressant as well. This should help him relax and make him feel better," said the first doctor.

"How long does all this take to be effective?" I asked.

"You usually see results within a couple of weeks but an actual proper diagnosis takes longer," said the second doctor. "It could take months."

"Are you kidding? Does Nick have to stay here that long?" I asked.

"I'm afraid so," said the first doctor. "Ultimately, we have to observe his behaviour over time and see how the various drugs take effect. We run several programs here in the Child and Adolescent ward with therapy sessions, as well as, there are qualified teachers on board to help keep the students on track with their school work so they don't miss any credits while they are in here."

"We can only do so much for Nick," said the second doctor. "We can prescribe the medication he needs but his family actually has the biggest part to play in his full recovery. It won't be easy but with a lot of patience and understanding, he should do well."

Doug and I went to visit Nick before we left for home. He looked pleased to see us but reserved. We explained to him about his treatment plan and how the doctors and nurses were here to help him feel better so that he could become well again and come home. We would come to visit him every day. We told him that he was allowed to call home from the pay phone outside of his room if he wanted to talk to us.

When we left, I felt exhausted from the emotion of the day. Doug and I reassured each other that Nick would be alright and that he was lucky to be well taken care of in the hospital. The next evening we brought Jennifer and Peter with us to visit Nick.

"Is he really crazy Mom?" said Peter on the way there.

"No Peter, why would you ask that?" I asked.

"I heard you and Dad talking about Nick hearing voices and how he's psychotic right? Well, that sounds crazy to me," he said.

"Yeah and now he's in the loony-bin," cried Jennifer.

"Nick is not crazy. He just has a chemical imbalance in his brain that needs to be corrected with medication. This will help him feel better and then he'll be able to come home. We all need to be nice to Nick and help him through all of this. Do you both understand?" I asked.

They both nodded but I could tell that they were really too young to comprehend what was going on in Nick's head and how this made him act crazy. I had to admit, I had no clue what was really going on in his mind either and what was causing him to act so crazy. We all had a lot to learn about mental illness.

Doug said to them, "When we go in to see Nick, just be yourself and show him that you care about him."

"Let's bring him some chocolate milk and some doughnuts. That'll make him feel better," suggested Peter.

"I'll make him a get well card too," said Jennifer.

"Those are great ideas. Nick will like that," I said.

After staying in the hospital for two and a half months, Nick was finally stable enough to come home. The doctors told us there would be an adjustment period for Nick going back to school and being in the outside world again. They emphasized that he had been through quite an ordeal and needed to remain on his medication as prescribed for life.

Various friends at school asked him where he had been. Some heard that he was sick with *Mononucleosis* and some said they thought that he had *Aids* while others even said that they thought he had died. The rumours flew all around high school but Nick handled it well by laughing it all off. He only told his best friend Curtis Brown what really happened to him and that he was bi-polar. Curtis told him that his mood disorder was no big deal to him. The hard part for Nick was getting through this time of adjustment and fitting in again with the crowd. He had missed two and a half months of grade nine with his friends and he said that he felt a little out of place with the in-crowd.

"I just want to feel normal again Mom," said Nick.

"That will take time Nick," I said to him. "You've been through a lot in the last few months. I'm just glad that you are doing so well now."

That was when Nick stopped taking all of his medication as prescribed and I didn't realize it until it was too late. As quickly as he went off the medication, he slipped into a catatonic state. He stopped eating, drinking and couldn't sleep. It was heart-breaking to see him in this state and I had no choice but to readmit him back in the hospital once again.

The doctor told us that it was typical of bi-polar patients to go off their medication once they started to feel well again. He went on to explain that as horrible as the lows were when the patient is down, they miss the ultimate highs of the mania too.

"What makes it so difficult to deal with is that although the medication stabilizes their mood, it also makes them feel flat, dull and almost lifeless in comparison," he said.

Nick had slipped dangerously fast into this state of mind where he was unresponsive and it was very terrifying to watch. It hit me twice as hard as the first time to see him like this and I wasn't sure I had the strength to go through all of this again. It was bad enough the first time Nick was unstable but this time it was more serious. Nick had reverted back to being in an infant-like state. He not only refused to eat and drink but he didn't even go to the washroom on his own.

When I asked the doctors what was happening to Nick, they couldn't say for sure other than he was in a catatonic state from suddenly going off his medication all at once. It was a shock to his system and it made him seem like he was in a trance. It was like a junkie going off drugs or an alcoholic jumping off the band wagon. It was considered to be a medical emergency and if left untreated it could result in death. If Nick didn't start to eat and drink within a few days' time, they would have to take him to the paediatric intensive care unit.

In the meantime, the doctors ordered more tests to see how the wave patterns were functioning in Nick's brain. When I took him down to have an MRI test done, I waited outside the testing room until Nick came back out. I smiled at him and he smiled back. Then he suddenly said, "Ah! That was really noisy Mom."

These were the first words that he had spoken in over a week and I said to him,"Nick you talked. That's wonderful."

Then he said to me, "Yeah, can you get me a *Gatorade* Mom? I'm really thirsty."

"Sure, whatever you want Nicky," I replied.

"Can I also go home now?" he asked. "I really don't like it in here at all."

"If you start to eat and drink and take your medication and stay on it, you sure can," I reassured him.

I asked the doctor why he suddenly had started to talk again.

"After all, you have to realize that *Bipolar Disorder* simply put is a brain disorder. The brain structure and function are altered in this condition and perhaps the noise of the MRI machine triggered a reaction in him. Years ago, electric shock therapy treatments were used on catatonic patients to jolt them back into reality," said the doctor. "You should feel fortunate that Nick reacted and has come out of that state of mind rather quickly."

It was such an overwhelming feeling to have Nick come back from what was a coma-like state. When he lost touch with reality, I had no idea how long he would be in that state. Luckily, his mind snapped out of the hold it was under and he returned to the real world and started to behave like a normal teenager again within a short period of time. Nick learned the hard way how important it was for him to take his medication on a regular basis and stay on the medication as prescribed by the doctor.

When Nick finally came home from the hospital this time, I made sure to celebrate his return and I promised him that I would do everything in my power to make sure that he never went back ever again.

CHAPTER SIXTEEN

Peter

Peter is precise. There's no other word that describes him better in my mind. He was always very intellectual and passionate about a lot of things from a very young age. He was very articulate too and spoke in full sentences by the time he reached eighteen months old and navigated the computer all by himself like an expert when he was only two years old. When he was three, he could name all the dinosaurs not only by their more common names but by their more appropriate Latin names as well. He taught himself to read before he went to kindergarten.

His teacher in kindergarten asked me, "Did you know that Peter could read? I have him reading to the grade one class," said his teacher.

As he grew up, Peter had several passions but music seemed to be one of his favourites. One day when he was eight years old, he started pounding on all the lids from the pots and pans with the wooden spoons in my kitchen. I knew then that he needed a set of drums. He seemed to be elated with his first drum set and pounded on them night and day. Even my neighbour commented one day, "He's improving."

"Sorry for all the noise," I replied.

"Oh, no worries," he said. "He sounds pretty good to me."

Then Peter wanted a guitar. He taught himself how to play the acoustic, bass and electric guitars. He downloaded the tabs from the internet and started to play different types of music from rock and roll to metal. He formed a band with some of his friends and started jamming over *Skype* on the internet. The technology allowed him to jam with on-line friends as far away as *Australia.* This gave Peter the advantage of playing music every day with different groups of musicians. This seemed to quench his appetite for music.

Peter too was an animal lover. We ended up having a zoo full of animals over the years. We had a blue-point Siamese cat named *Meowser,* a tri-coloured guinea pig named *Saboo,* a fire sand bearded dragon named *Draca* and a tiger stripped Gecko named *Cleo.*

He had a true love for animals and said that he wanted to become a naturalist when he grew up so that he could study the behaviour of animals in the wild. He was only four years old when I caught him in a peculiar position while we were camping up in northern *Ontario.* He had dug a hole in the sand on our campsite and put several pebbles in the bottom of the hole. He then lay down over top of the hole and started to move like he was *humping* the hole. When he got up, I asked him, "What are you doing Peter?" I tried not to laugh too hard as I giggled. I looked at Doug and he too was laughing at this point.

"I'm fertilizing the eggs Mom," said Peter seriously.

I knew then that Peter not only had a love for animals but that he knew all about their characteristics and behaviours from a very young age.

"How does he know all about fertilization?" I asked Doug later on that night.

"He has obviously watched all those nature shows on the *Discovery* channel very carefully," said Doug. "As far as that humping part goes, he's a chip off the old block!"

Peter was also very protective of the wild and was always ready to save any animal from harm. When Peter was only eight years old, he saw a group of older boys throwing rocks at a group of ducks in the lake at camp. He hopped on his bike and went looking for the Park Warden to tell her what he had seen. The Warden thanked him and noticed that he looked very unhappy about the kids hurting the wild animals.

"I hope you are not worried about squealing on those kids," said the Warden.

"Are you kidding?" he asked rather boldly. "I only feel bad for the ducks and those kids are the ones that are going to feel bad after I'm done with them."

"You did the right thing by coming here to tell me about what you saw. You spoke up for the animals that can't. If I catch them, they can be fined," she said to him.

Peter was very sensitive when it came to the wild. When he snagged a snapping turtle on his fishing line by mistake up at *Rock Lake* in *Algonquin Park*, he became vividly upset. He threw down his bike when he arrived back at camp and started to cry. When I asked him what was wrong, he told me about snagging the snapping turtle on his line. He told me that he was worried that he gave the turtle a death sentence.

"But the turtle won't be able to eat and she'll die. It's my entire fault," said Peter.

"She should be alright," I said to Peter. "Turtles don't have a reputation for living to a ripe old age for nothing."

When the Warden came by our camp, I told her how upset Peter was about snagging the snapper and I asked her to try to console him. She went on to tell him that they had caught and tagged many turtles in their research studies over the years and many had hook marks in their lips and this did not stop them from eating and they all had survived without any problems.

Peter continued to rescue all sorts of animals at home as well as at camp. This included rabbits, chipmunks, snakes, frogs and even a little salamander that popped out of the wood pile one day. He wanted to rehabilitate all wild animals that needed help and release them back in the wild once he thought they were ready to return to their natural habitat.

When we all camped at *Algonquin Park*, it was the world famous *Wolf Howl* that became Peter's favourite experience. It was quiet a thrill to hear the naturalists howl for the wolves in the middle of the night and to have the wild wolves howl back.

Nick joked that it was all a hoax and that the naturalists had a tape recorder in the field with the sounds of wolves that they played for the crowds that attended.

"The whole thing is a fake," Nick said to Peter.

"You're wrong Nick," said Peter as he tried to wrestle with Nick but he held him back. "You wouldn't know a real wolf howl from a fake one anyway. People come from all over the world to hear the park rangers howl at the wolves once they locate the wolves and their pups. It's amazing to hear the wolves and their pups reply."

"Yeah, whatever," said Nick. "I heard it before and it's no big deal."

It was rather obvious that Nick didn't have a love for animals like Peter did. Peter had a connection with animals and his favourite animal of all was our black and white *Alaskan Husky* dog named

Shila. She was a rescue dog that we adopted at four months of age. She was wolf-like and loved to pull the kids on their sleds around the block in the winter time. All you had to say was the magic word *go* and she would take off like a rocket.

Peter liked to play fight with his dog all the time until shortly after he turned twelve years old. I started seeing a disturbing trend in his behaviour that included loosing interest in playing with *Shila.* He was saying that he felt down for no reason. He not only lost interest in his pets but worst of all, he stopped playing music. The red flags went up and it all started to sound very familiar after what I had gone through with Nick. Peter was very irritable and wouldn't get up for school in the morning either. His behaviour worsened day by day up until the day that I noticed he had carved the words *I hate you* in the head board of his bed. When I asked him who he hated, he said very coldly, "You!"

This simple word shot through me like a knife. *Was it all happening again?* I asked myself. I felt fortunate that Nick was stabilized on medication and that he was back to living a normal teenage life. *Could Peter be afflicted with the same disorder as his older brother?* I questioned myself. I knew that they each had some of the same genes on my side of the family but they had different fathers. *What were the odds of both of them having the same illness?* I questioned. I knew I had to do something the day that I came home from work and found Peter curled up on the little couch in the living room. He didn't speak at first when I asked him why he was curled up like that. He was curled in the fetal position and he looked frightened.

I caressed his face and asked him to tell me what was wrong. He simply said, "Go look in my closet and you'll find out." When I went to his room, I was horrified to see the cord from his fan fashioned into the shape of a noose. I knew then that he needed help.

Doug and I brought Peter to the same psychiatrist that Nick had seen and explained all the problems that he was experiencing in the last months. It didn't take much to be diagnosed with bi-polar disorder as well. Both the doctor and nurse said that we were very observant parents to bring Peter in and not to have ignored the deadly signs that he portrayed. It was their experience that a lot of parents either ignored the signs of trouble not believing something was actually wrong with their child or some people just did not know what the signs were of this illness in the first place. Doug and I had the experience and I truly believe that we avoided more serious problems that could have otherwise developed for Peter had we not had this experience.

After Peter was on medication for his illness and when he was feeling better one day, I asked him, "You don't really hate me do you Pete?"

"No Mom, of course not," he said sheepishly. "It's just sometimes I need to be left alone. When I'm in a really down mood, it doesn't matter what happens around me. I hate everything, including myself. I know now that it is a struggle within me to come to terms with my moods and to try to stay positive. I really do love you Mom and Dad too for all the help."

Peter's moods stabilized over time but there were triggers in his life that would bring him down to that dark place of depression. He told me that it felt like there was this ugly monster that slowly but meticulously crept up on him and grabbed a hold of him with a tight grip. I had to be careful to recognize what the triggers were and make sure that he did not suck any of us down with him into this vortex. At times when Peter was being difficult, I tried talking and discussing his defiance with my authority in a calm manner but then I usually ended up yelling and screaming out of frustration. I tried everything in my power which included punishing, pleading and negotiating to try to get through to him. There was a fine line in trying to be sensitive to his needs while trying to keep the rest of the family happy as well. As my mother used to say in reference to Maria, she was only as happy as her unhappiest child. This was so true for me as well when it came to Peter. It made me so sad to see him when he was in that dark ugly place and when he was down his behaviour affected the entire family.

Jennie who was happy most of the time said to me, "It breaks my heart to see him this way Mom. He seems to withdraw from the whole world including his family. If only there was something that we could do for him to help him get out of that black hole."

"We can try until we are blue in the face," I said. "He is the only one who can bring himself out of that frame of mind. His lack of motivation is quite possibly his most inhibiting weakness and he will have to find a way to make the first move to crawl out on his own and then we can be there to help him along the way if he asks for our help."

As Peter learned how to bring himself back to reality, he was back to drumming and strumming and enjoying his pets again. Over time, he became more self confident and independent. Peter even started to socialize more even though he admitted that he had a bit of social anxiety when it came to being around a crowd of people.

"I just want to belong and I'm not going to let this illness stop me from achieving my goals Mom," said Peter. "I feel terrified at times to leave the safety net of home and enter the outside world. High school is a scary place filled with so many eyes upon me that I feel everyone is starring and judging me all the time."

Peter had to learn to deal with his anxiety and we all needed to learn to have lots of patience with him. It was good for Peter to use his talent that he had in music to create a band with friends from school and start jamming on weekends. He had tryouts for band members and if anyone did any illegal drugs, they were out of the band. Peter had a select number of friends who did not allow drugs to get in the way of their creativity.

I truly believe that if left untreated, Peter's illness was a disaster waiting to happen. Peter became very sensitive to other people's feelings and even helped out a friend who had suicidal thoughts one day. He wouldn't tell me who the friend was since that was confidential and I didn't expect him to. I just advised him to make sure that his friend was safe from harm and that if he needed adult help, just to ask.

"Do this person's parents know that their child has these thoughts?" I asked Peter.

"Yes, they do. I think my friend is going to be alright. My friend was on a certain medication that the doctors changed and this made them unstable and it was making her have these thoughts," said Peter. "It's mostly because I have had experience with this myself that I can be of help to her."

"You are being a great friend by supporting this person Pete," I said to him. "Just make sure you don't get yourself in too deep with this problem and leave the major part of this up to the doctors and the parents."

"I will Mom," said Peter. "Don't worry."

It turned out that the person who was having problems was Peter's new girlfriend, Sky Collins. She was a petite girl with beautiful eyes and a great singing voice. She had been in the hospital in the past for problems with *anorexia* but was struggling to be healthy again. This too was considered a mental illness that needed treatment with great care. It was good for both Peter and Sky to share their experiences and support each other in their teenage years.

When I thought about my own children, I started to wonder why they had been afflicted with mental illness. There was such a social stigma attached to this type of illness. *What were the environmental factors, if any that may have contributed to the illness? Were we doing something wrong to make them this way?* I asked myself.

It didn't take me long to conclude that it was indeed the heredity factor that was the mitigating factor. You couldn't do anything about your genetics. It was a curse whether you inherited cancer or mental illness. It was how you dealt with the illness that makes a difference in the quality of your life. When I thought about the moods that my father had, those of my sister Maria, my brother Matt and both Nick and Peter, all I could think of now was Jennie. *Was she next in line to receive this curse?*

CHAPTER SEVENTEEN

Jennie

Jennifer was just a few months older than little Megan Walker at the time that Megan died. Even though they had gone to different schools, they had played soccer together on the same team and had taken ballet lessons together too. Jennifer was having a hard time dealing with the death of her friend and neighbour after Megan had passed away.

"Why did she have to die Mom?" asked Jennifer.

"God has a plan for all of us and we don't know what that is. It is our faith in him that helps us get through tragedies like this. It doesn't seem fair though does it?" I tried to explain to her.

"No. I miss her Mom," said Jennifer.

"The best way to keep her close is to keep her in your heart Jennie," I said.

This seemed to console her and I found that children understood things better if you spoke to them from the heart.

Jennie had a very sweet disposition and although she was shy when she was very young and stuck to my side, she grew in confidence with her abilities as she turned ten. She seemed to excel at whatever she tried, whether it was ballet, soccer, gymnastics, volleyball or drama. She was also a great student in school with a straight *A* average.

When her kindergarten teacher said that she wished that she had twenty-one Jennie's in her class, I asked, "Wouldn't that be boring to have them all the same?"

"Oh no," she said rather coyly, "It would be lovely. It would make my job a lot easier."

Jennie was creative and developed into a very good artist. She started drawing and painting at a young age and it wasn't until one day that Uncle Ronald came for a visit and commented that the art on the fridge was improving, that I thought to myself, *well of course she's a girl who takes greater care in her artwork than the boys ever did.*

I took closer notice when in grade seven she won the contest for best art design of the yearbook cover. The theme that everyone was asked to portray was Friendship. She simply drew the hands of five of her friends with their index and fore fingers each in the form of a peace sign arranged in a circular fashion forming a star. She explained that as long as there was peace among friends there was hope to have peace in this world. As it turned out, years later she would blossom into a real artist.

Now there were times when Jennie showed another side of her personality like the time she was only two years old and I had put her in her room for a time-out for not listening to me. She started to scream at the top of her lungs and pounded on the door so hard that she almost went through it. I discussed my concerns about her temper tantrums with Doug but as she was only two at the time and since she was able to calm herself down, I dismissed it to being the terrible two syndromes. I thought that having a temper could also be a positive trait since it also gave her a fierce determination that she never got pushed around by anyone.

By the time she was eight years old, she would just walk up to any bully in the school yard and tell them to leave whoever they were picking on alone or she would show them. Since she was taller than all the boys, she only had to warn them with a jester that really wasn't very lady-like and they would stop in their tracks. They respected her for not letting anyone push her around and this allowed her to stand up for the under-dog.

Jennie grew fast and surpassed Peter in height by the time she was in grade eight. She liked telling people, "This is my little brother," even though she was younger.

She woke up in the middle of the night with growing pains in her legs. One night when I heard her sobs that sounded like they were more severe than normal, I went to see her. After the whole experience of our neighbour Megan and her appendix bursting, I didn't hesitate to take her to the hospital even though it was two o'clock in the morning.

Her pains would come and go, so the nurse that we saw first dismissed my concern that it might be appendicitis and thought that she was only constipated. After a two hour wait, the emergency room doctor dismissed her pains as appendicitis as well and suggested we visit our family doctor if the pains persisted so that we could be referred to a specialist. For weeks her pains continued and seemed to be the worst in the middle of the night.

When Doug brought Jennie to her appointment with our family doctor, I had written down on a piece of paper, a list of possible problems that I thought she could have ranging from *lactose intolerance, irritable bowel syndrome* or *Celiac Disease.*

Doug told me that when he handed the list to our doctor, she said to him, "Let's see what Doctor Jeanette thinks."

Doug told me that he chuckled and said to our doctor, "You know how a mother can be when there's something wrong with one of her babies. Jeanette thought especially that it was likely Jennie had

Celiac Disease since her niece was diagnosed with this disease last year at about the same age Jennie is now."

Doug went on to tell me that our doctor said, "Well, she could be right about that. You know a mother's instinct is usually right and *Celiac Disease* is hereditary. She wants to start off with a simple blood test to determine that and see what else might be causing the problems that Jennie has been experiencing. She suggested that if we need to do other tests, we can do that later."

Sure enough when the doctor called back with the results of Jennie's blood test, we were told that it came back positive for *Celiac Disease*. Since there was no cure for this disease, except to stay on a gluten-free diet for the rest of her life, the doctor recommended that Jennie undergo a biopsy of the small intestine to confirm the test results. We were told that sometimes blood tests were not always accurate and it was better to confirm the disease though a biopsy.

It turned out that the biopsy confirmed beyond a doubt that Jennie indeed had *Celiac Disease*. It is a wheat intolerance that if left undiagnosed could lead to mal-absorption of vitamins and minerals in the body that in turn leads to various health problems over time such as anemia, osteoporosis, nerve damage, infertility, muscle weakness and even cancer.

This brought back painful memories of my mother who suffered from *Osteoporosis* and who died from cancer. Perhaps she had *Celiac Disease* that caused her other medical conditions but just never knew it. I read that symptoms of this disease vary among patients with some showing little or no signs of the disease at all.

I was glad that I found out at a young age that in order to combat *Celiac Disease* and stay healthy, Jennie only had to stick to a strict gluten-free diet to prevent future health issues. This meant extra work in baking and cooking separate meals for Jennie but it was worth it. Soon enough she learnt how to cook and bake for herself and we all tried some of the foods that Jennie had to eat and found that some items like gluten-free pancakes actually tasted better than regular pancakes made with wheat flour. It was an adjustment we all had to make but it really wasn't that difficult compared to the adjustment that our neighbours had to make down the street.

Jennie always ate healthy and stuck to her special diet and blossomed into a beautiful young girl with her long black hair, slim figure and dynamite smile. She always seemed to be very responsible for her age and became fiercely independent as puberty set in. When she turned thirteen, she asked if she could go to a *MVD* dance in downtown *London* with a few of her friends.

"What's that?" I asked Jennie. "*Much Video Dance*," she explained. "It's a great place to go dancing with your friends. It's held downtown at *Centennial Hall* from seven until ten on Friday nights. There are security guards there to make sure everything is safe. Can I go, please?"

"It sounds like trouble to me," said Doug. "Anything with initials like that *MVD*, '*Much Venereal Disease*' doesn't sound like a good place for our daughter to be."

"I don't think it's a good idea to let her go to that Mom," said Peter. "The kids that go there are all underage drinkers and sluts."

"It's not like that at all," exclaimed Jennie. "You don't know what you're talking about Peter. You're just jealous because you don't have as many friends as I do."

"I have lots of good friends, not like you and those slut girl friends of yours," he said.

"Peter, cut it out and leave Jennie alone," I said. "I know you are only trying to look out for your sister but she's a good girl and just wants to have some fun."

"Yeah, what kind of fun?" asked Peter sarcastically.

"Mom, it's not like that. Peter is acting stupid and I wish he would just leave me alone," cried Jennie.

"Okay, Jennie. I'll let you go because I trust you," I said. "I'll give you Dad's phone so that you can call if you need to. Promise that you won't leave the building until I come to pick you up at ten."

"I promise," said Jennie. "Nothing bad will happen."

I did have some apprehensions about letting Jennie go to this much video dance downtown once I found out that there were approximately eight hundred other pre-teens that gathered at this dance. Peter told me that he heard that there were a lot of kids that would get high or drunk and make out at these dances.

"You shouldn't let her go," Peter said to me later in confidence. "She's hanging around with those slut girlfriends of hers and I don't want to see her go down that same path, that's all."

"Peter, I trust your sister," I said to him. "She will be fine. I know it's not your scene but she likes to dance so I don't see the harm."

Friday night came and I dropped Jennie and two of her girlfriends off at the dance. When it was ten o'clock, I was back there to pick them up again but didn't see them at first so I called Jennie on the cell phone but it went right to voice mail. Now I waited impatiently and became annoyed as I didn't see the girls coming through the dance doors. I saw several other parents waiting as well but they all found their children and escorted them to their cars.

As I waited for Jennie and her friends, I heard a young girl say to one of her friends, "I wish I could have made out with Ryan tonight. He's so cute." Her girlfriend replied," "No, Matt is way cuter."

By this time, I had heard enough and finally Jennie and her friends came out of the dance. I looked at them and immediately asked Jennie what was wrong since she looked as white as a ghost and I noticed that one of her friends had a cold compress on her nose.

"Dad's phone is missing. Someone took it," said Jennie. "Alica here got punched in the face by some bitch."

"What kind of talk is that Jennie? This is the exact reason why your father and I hesitated to let you go to this dance," I said to her. "Are you alright Alicia? What happened?"

"I'm alright. It hurts a little," said Alicia. "Some stupid girl thought I was stealing her boyfriend when he asked me to dance so she punched me. She got kicked out of the dance by security. I'm not sure what my Mom will say."

"Well, I know what I have to say. That's it, no more! This is the first and the last time Jennie will be going here!" I said very sternly. "Did you find out if they have a lost and found here?"

"Yes, we did and no-one has turned it in," said Jennie.

"That's an expensive phone Jennie and your Dad needs it for work and to top it all off, it's our Anniversary tonight. Now once Dad finds out, he'll be very upset," I said to her. At that moment, Doug called me on my cell phone from home to see why it was taking so long to pick-up the girls.

"They were searching for your phone. It was stolen by some little moron," I said to him.

"Well, that figures," said Doug. "I told you those dances were nothing but trouble. Well, don't come home without it." He hung up and all I could think of was that I would be hung up too once I got home.

When we arrived home, I could see that Doug was still furious that his phone was missing. He looked red in the face and grumbled. Later that evening Doug said to me, "I guess worse things could have happened tonight, if some guy had hurt Jennie or tried anything with her. I'd kill him," he said. "Then I'd be in jail and what kind of an anniversary would that be?"

"No good obviously," I replied. "I told Jennie that she's grounded and she will have to pay us back for the phone. She felt really bad about the phone being stolen. It's a shame that kids who steal these phones just don't care at all about the inconvenience of not having your phone and the expense to replace it."

"There's another four-hundred and fifty dollars down the drain," said Doug. "They'll probably end up buying a new SIM card for the phone and selling it for a hundred bucks to someone all at our expense."

"The security lady at the hall said that at least two phones go missing every weekend at these dances," I said. "We'll get you a new phone in the morning. In the meantime, HAPPY ANNIVERSARY!"

"Yeah, some anniversary this turned out to be," Doug said. "Let's go to bed baby and make up for this!"

The passion was hot between us that night as we caressed each other and held each other tight. Later on in the evening I asked Doug, "How are we going to get through these teenage years?"

"I don't know, honey," he said as he stroked my back. "I think we have to do a lot of praying and hope that we instilled the right values in our children for them to make the right decisions in life."

"That is the hope of course," I replied. "We'll just have to keep one step ahead of them. They are all good kids but they still need a lot of guidance. I'm not sure how my parents got through the teenage years with five kids."

As Doug stroked my lips and kissed me very gently, he said, "And they said it wouldn't last. It's been seventeen wonderful years honey. It's our anniversary tonight so let's forget about the kids for a while," he said as he started to kiss me all over. "Let's make love again and see if you still respect me in the morning."

I thought that Doug was right, that we just had to see what happened next. I knew we were in for many more adventures but hopefully, we instilled the right values in our children. I hoped that they would make the right choices in life or at the very least learn from the wrong ones.

The following weekend, Jennie made plans to go out to the movies with two of her friends. She told us that she was going to take the bus there so that we didn't have to drive her and she would be back, before curfew. She said that she was sorry again for loosing Dad's phone the weekend before. Doug and I had both decided to let her go on the promise that she would come home right after the movie was over.

After Jennie left, Doug and I went for a ride on his motorcycle and went past the bus stop where we saw Jennie and her friends hitch-hiking. Doug immediately pulled over at the bus stop and told the girls to wait there while he made a phone call. Within two minutes a police cruiser pulled up to the bus stop where the girls were standing. When Doug shook the officer's hand and asked the girls to get in the back of the cruiser, they looked horrified.

"Don't worry," Doug said to the girls. "You're not under arrest but I have asked Officer Duncan to escort you somewhere and we will follow."

As the girls got in the police cruiser, I asked Doug what he was doing. He just told me to wait and see. The girls looked a little bit nervous and I didn't really know what was going to unfold next. The police car went down a familiar road and stopped in the library parking lot not too far from home. Doug asked the girls to get out and waved thanks to the officer as she left. The girls looked relieved but perplexed.

"Now girls, please come with us into the library. I want to show you something," he said very calmly to them. They didn't say a word or ask any questions but they simply followed him.

"I think I have their full attention," whispered Doug to me.

"It looks like it," I replied.

Doug had the girls gather around the computer terminal and asked Jennie to sit down and look up the name Suzy Lindenberg on the *London Free Press* internet website. As Jennie googled the name, the girls watched as the headline read, *June 12th, 2005, Suzy Lindenberg raped and murdered.* When Jennie clicked on the link, a full page story appeared along with a picture of a beautiful young girl that looked remarkably similar to Jennie. They all gasped.

"Alright now, I want each one of you to read a paragraph out loud from this story starting with you Cassie," said Doug.

"But we're in the library Dad, we can't read this out loud," protested Jennie.

"I don't care, please read," he demanded.

Cassie began to read the first paragraph that read, *London, June 12th, 2005—Suzy Lindenberg was found raped and murdered last night in a woodlot outside London. Her attacker is believed to be a white male in his early twenties with short black hair, around five foot eight tall and weighing 160 pounds. Police are still investigating the crime.*

"Paula, you're next please," said Doug.

Paula began to read the second paragraph out loud; *Suzy was fourteen years old and attended St. Thomas Moore High School. She will be dearly missed by her mother and father and two older brothers. Suzy was a bright, energetic and artistic young girl.*

"Now, it's your turn Jennie. Please read the last paragraph of the article," Doug said.

Jennie began to read slowly, *it is believed that Suzy had been hitch-hiking with two friends on the night she disappeared. She was snatched . . .* Jennie couldn't finish reading the sentence, so Doug finished it . . . *by the attacker while her two friends watched helplessly. The police have issued a warning to be on the lookout for a dark blue pick-up truck with mag wheels that the attacker drove. Anyone with any information about this crime should call the police or crime stoppers.*

By this time, all three girls were crying and the librarian had come over to see what was happening. She looked over and asked if everything was alright. Doug told her he was giving the girls a lesson in the perils of hitch-hiking. She nodded and seemed to understand when she glanced at the article up on the screen.

Doug told the girls to wait in the library until we went home to pick up the car and I would come back to give each of the girls a safe ride home. He asked them if we should tell their parents that they were hitch-hiking but they all agreed that it wouldn't be necessary and that they had learnt their lesson. Jennie was quiet and didn't say anything along the way until her friends were dropped off. Once we got home and as she got out of the vehicle and approached Doug as he was waiting for her in the driveway, she ran up to him, gave him a big hug and said, "I hope you're not too mad at me Dad. I won't ever hitch-hike again. It was very stupid of me wasn't it?"

"Well, I sure hope you'll never do that again. When you're young, you think you are infallible but you need to be smart with your choices. You only have one life to live and it's very precious. I hope you learned your lesson today honey," he said to her.

"Yes, I did Dad," she said.

Chapter Eighteen

Lucky Man

The day arrived that I had to take Doug to the hospital to have a blood transfusion after our family doctor had taken his blood pressure and found it to be so dangerously low. Doug had gone to see the doctor that day for a routine medical check-up to renew his AZ truck driver license.

"She asked me how I've been feeling lately," said Doug when he called me to pick him up from the doctor's office.

"What are you talking about?" I asked.

"I told her that I was feeling with my hands," joked Doug. "She got mad at me and I had to admit to her that I haven't been feeling too shit hot lately. She took my blood pressure twice and said that it is very low. She thinks I might be bleeding internally and that I might have an ulcer. She also insists that I need a blood transfusion. If you don't come to pick me up right away to take me to the hospital, then she said she will call an ambulance to have them take me there. I failed my physical so she won't let me drive at all right now."

"I'll be right there," I said. "Don't even think about moving."

When I picked Doug up from the doctor's office and drove him to the hospital, it took several hours of waiting before the emergency room doctor came and took Doug's blood pressure and ordered blood work to be done. He told us that although his blood pressure

125

was low, it was his opinion that a blood transfusion was not necessary at this time and that it would only mask the problem before he knew what the real problem was with his haemoglobin. He didn't seem to be as concerned as our family doctor was about Doug's condition. He told us to go home, even though it was one thirty in the morning and to come back the next day for more tests.

I was confused and worried but we came back the next day to have more tests completed including an ultrasound test in the morning and a scheduled endoscope test to be done in the afternoon. While in the waiting room at the hospital, I received a call on my cell phone from our family doctor about the results of Doug's ultrasound test that morning. I left the room to take the call outside and she said to me, "I know why Doug's blood pressure is so low. It looks like he has a lesion on his pancreas. The ultrasound shows a shadow of a mass the size of eleven centimetres."

I was caught off guard with the news and asked, "A lesion? What is that caused by?" I asked this question before I really had the chance to think about the answer.

The line was quiet and there was no answer from my doctor. My heart skipped a beat as I slowly asked, "Oh, its cancer isn't it?" Instantly, I could feel all the blood drain out of my face.

After what seemed like an eternity, my doctor simply replied, "We can't say that for sure but I can tell you that whatever it is, Doug does have a long road ahead of him."

I went back into the waiting room and tried to muster up the strength to tell Doug what the doctor had told me. *How would I tell him this news?* I questioned myself. *Maybe it was best not to say anything to him at this time until after all the test results came in and there were more conclusive results. There was no use in shocking him any more than I was already.*

When I slowly walked over to talk to Doug, there was no hiding my ghostly exterior. When Doug saw me, he immediately asked me, "Who called and what's wrong?"

My mind raced with the thought that this could be a mistake. The doctors had looked at the wrong ultrasound chart. This wasn't happening to Doug, it must be someone else's chart but I came to the realization that there was no mistake and I had no choice but to blurt out the truth.

"It's a lesion," I said. "The ultrasound test shows that it's on your pancreas."

Doug looked expressionless. He only said, "Oh."

"We'll know more once you have this endoscope test done," I said. "Let's not jump to any conclusions."

All I could think of at that moment was that my mother had died from a lesion on her pancreas and this was a dead sentence. The endoscope procedure that was done in the afternoon revealed that the mass looked like it was sitting on the top his stomach. We went home that night and tried to reassure each other that everything was going to be fine. I made sure Doug was asleep before I balled my eyes out. I prayed that we would get through this ordeal and that Doug wouldn't die. I needed him and so did the children. I didn't want to be a single mother again. *Was it selfish of me to think that?* I asked myself as I cried myself to sleep.

A few days later, we had an appointment to see a surgeon. It was all moving so fast yet I felt like I was in a daze. Doctor Maynard was a very well spoken man in his early fifties who gave off an heir of confidence that I found refreshing, although the news that he gave us did not.

"From looking at the ultrasound, it's hard to say for sure but I think you have a rare form of cancer called a *sarcoma*. It's a *GIST* (*Gastrointestinal Stromal Tumour*) that is a slow growth, soft tissue cancer," he said matter of fact. It hit me like a ton of bricks. Even though I had seen first-hand what cancer does to people, I was not prepared to hear this type of news. I only knew then that I *hated* cancer.

"I will have to operate to remove the growth but I won't know what it's attached to until I open you up. The growth is large and it seems to be sitting on the outside of your stomach and could be attached to various vital organs including your main arteries, your spleen and or your pancreas," he went on to say.

It sure sounded like a death sentence to me but I didn't want to let Doug know what I was thinking. Instead I asked, "How soon can you operate?"

"I will send you to the oncologist first to see if he thinks we should try to shrink this tumour before operating," said Doctor Maynard. "There's a new drug that inhibits this type of tumour. If we shrink it, it will be easier to remove. We also need to do a biopsy to verify that this is indeed a *GIST*."

I looked at Doug and saw the disappointment on his face about the news we were hearing. This news was devastating. *Why was this happening to us?* I asked myself. Doug was only forty-eight years old and had this growth dwelling inside of him festering for at least the last four years, according to what the doctor went on to tell us.

"I'd rather die from lead-poisoning and get it over with right now," Doug groaned. He was referring to what my father had always said about his buddies who died in the war. They had been shot with bullets made from lead; hence they died from lead poisoning.

I found that the toughest part in the battle against cancer was the mental battle rather than the mere physical battle itself. I noticed that people in general seemed to be able to deal with the pain and sickness of the disease a lot easier than the emotional stress of the disease that carried with it the greatest challenge.

As we left the doctor's office, Doug asked, "What about going camping in *Algonquin Park* this summer? I'm not sure we'll be able to go with this damn tumour inside of me. Every bump on the road is painful and it's a long way to travel."

"We'll have to skip going to *Algonquin* for one year Doug," I said sadly. "It's more important that you rest and keep up your strength for the operation. We'll have many more years ahead to look forward to going to *Algonquin* after you've had your surgery."

"I don't care. Come hell or high water, we're going to *Algonquin* this summer," said Doug. "It could be my last."

Within a couple of days, we were back in the hospital for the biopsy and as the nurses were prepping him for the procedure, I happened to look at his chart that read, biopsy—liver.

"What is this, biopsy—liver?" I questioned.

"We are preparing him for a biopsy," said one of the nurses.

"Not on his liver!" I exclaimed. "The tumour is on his stomach. You had better call Dr. Maynard right now to confirm."

The nurses looked perplexed as I questioned the orders but I insisted that I wasn't going to let them take Doug for the biopsy until they confirmed the order with the doctor. Sure enough, they called Dr. Maynard and he confirmed that the procedure was to perform the biopsy on the tumour located on the stomach. The nurse said that he was livid that someone had written the wrong order on the chart and he told her to re-write the order to complete the biopsy of the tumour on his stomach.

"You have to be your own best advocate when it comes to your health. Everyone makes mistakes, but this type could have been fatal," I said to Doug.

"I'm glad I have you looking out for me Jeanette," said Doug. "I can't even imagine what the results would be if they had done a biopsy on the wrong part."

"My pleasure," I said. "We have to go see another specialist now at the cancer clinic. Have you had enough of doctors and tests yet?"

When we first arrived at the cancer clinic, it was so overwhelming to see so many sick people sitting there waiting to see doctors and specialists for their varying treatments and appointments. Some people had bandanas over their heads while others were completely bald. Seeing the sick children though gave me the worst feeling. It was a gloomy place that I would have to visit with Doug many more times in the years ahead and it was a place that I never got comfortable being in.

When it was finally our turn to see the oncologist, Dr. Levian, he told us that although the type of cancer Doug had was rare, less than one percent of all cancers fell within this type, there was a new drug called *Gleevec* that was only available in *Canada* for use against this type of cancer within the last year. He recommended that Doug start on this drug right away and shrink the tumour before surgery. I had many questions for him, including, "How long would it take to shrink the tumour? What was the dosage required? What are the side effects of this drug? How much does it cost? How effective is this drug in the treatment of this type of cancer?"

He answered, "It will take between four to eight months to shrink the tumour. The side effects are nausea, vomiting, diarrhea and weight loss. The dose is one oral 400mg pill per day. It is a very expensive drug that costs around one hundred dollars a day. We know that in trials, this drug has been very effective in the treatment of this type of cancer. The rate of success is unknown since it is so new to the market here in *Canada*."

So there it was all the facts of treatment and prognosis in a nutshell. I had so many other questions but couldn't think of them at that moment. It was all so much to absorb and emotionally, it was draining.

Doug started his daily chemotherapy treatment and the tumour started slowly shrinking. It was difficult to imagine that Doug had such a large growth that slowly grew over many years to the size of a grapefruit and now it was slowly but more quickly shrinking down in size. This gave me hope that the tumour was dying and the battle against cancer could possibly be won. There was still the thought of going through surgery to remove the tumour still looming but I told Doug that we had to take things one day at a time. Doug started looking pale and weak in those days of treatment before he had his surgery.

Dr. Levian seemed elated though that the *Gleevec* pill had shrunk the tumour from eleven centimetres down to seven centimetres in size within an eight month period. I got the feeling that Doug was just a guinea pig to him though. It wasn't that he didn't seem to care about his patient and how he was feeling but he just seemed more thrilled that the experimental drug was actually working despite how the side effects made Doug feel. Eight months earlier, he had been really concerned that Doug was bleeding internally from the tumour and that he needed to start treatment at that time or he would have only had a month and a half to live. It was a real shock to hear that Doug was so close to death and we both were not even aware of it at the time.

"We'll make you into a new man," said Dr. Levian. "You are a very lucky man to be standing here in front of me right now." Ironic, how the doctor described it, that Doug was a lucky man.

How lucky was he that he had cancer in the first place? I questioned myself. *How lucky was he that he still needed surgery to remove this tumour? How lucky was he that he had to take this chemotherapy pill that made him feel sick every day? How lucky was he?*

Furthermore, Dr. Levian told us that in order to inhibit the cancer from coming back after surgery; Doug had to stay on the *Gleevec* for the rest of his life. That meant feeling sick for the rest of his life too. *For how many years could a person's body take this poison? If he was so lucky, would the nausea, pain and vomiting ever go away?* I questioned myself.

Although I was thankful that Doug was still here, alive, I certainly would not have described him as being a lucky man. I did have to admit to myself though that Doug was lucky that the *Gleevec* stopped his internal bleeding and this allowed us to go to *Algonquin Park* that summer. Doug was determined to go camping and so we left for our vacation even though he was in a lot of pain.

I must say that I was happiest when we were on the road again, especially during our family camping trips. We had camped at almost every provincial park within a six-hour distance from *London* starting when the kids were babies. When we circled on the map the number of camps that we had been to over the years, it came to twenty-two different parks. Nothing compared to *Algonquin Park* though where we camped every year since the kids were old enough to hike. Our favourite camp within the park was *Rock Lake* which was nestled quietly off the main highway. As we took the eight kilometer dirt road from the main highway corridor into the camp entrance and drove over the old train bridge, all my troubles seemed to disappear for a while. Arriving in paradise had made the long six and a half hour journey from *London* all worth it.

After our departure from *Algonquin's* beauty, it was back to reality though and a gruelling five hour operation to remove Doug's tumour four months later. Dr. Maynard cut Doug open from his breast bone down to just below his belly button and left a scar, seven inches long. He removed the tumour along with a few other parts that were infested with the cancer and reconnected the digestive tract as best as he could.

Before surgery, I was with Doug as he pleaded with the doctor to save some of his stomach so that he wouldn't have to be put on a feeding tube for the rest of his life. He told the doctor that if he didn't have a stomach left, then he couldn't eat properly and there was really no point then in living. Dr. Maynard sympathized with him but he reiterated that he wouldn`t know for sure what organs were infested with the cancer until he opened him up. Through the great skill of the doctor though, Doug had his spleen, his gall bladder and only two-thirds of his stomach removed during the operation. The doctor was able to save one-third of his stomach.

"He saved part of your stomach," I said to Doug after he came to from his operation. "What a lucky man you are!"

And this time, I mean it! I thought to myself.

CHAPTER NINETEEN
Seth & Emily

While we were going through hell with the battle against cancer, Maria was going through hell with her battle with both of her children, Seth and Emily. She was on her own dealing with all the troubles that followed after Andrew committed suicide. To get a glimpse into the mind of my nephew Seth, you need only read what he wrote on his on-line wall when he was ten years old that read:

The reason people use a crucifix against vampires is that vampires are allergic to bullshit.

He was a troubled child from day one. Maria told me that he was known all over town in *Ottawa* as the '*NO boy*' when he was only two years old. He was a very cute boy at that age as all children are and wherever she went, people would ask him what his name was. He blurted out, "*No*" with an angry-looking face.

He stood in front of the television while we tried to watch, stuck out his arms and yelled, "*NO!*" He never got out of the way freely. Maria had to pry him away.

As he got a little older, he constantly terrorized kids at the playground where he lived and threw sand in their faces and laughed at them when they started to cry. He was uncontrollable all the way through elementary school and spent his final year of grade eight with his desk parked outside the principal's office. Needless to say he didn't have many friends other than a couple of unruly misfits along the way. He was mean to his younger sister Emily too even though he always said that he adored her.

Maria tried correcting his behaviour in many ways through discipline and brought him from one child psychologist to another to have him analyzed and to see what treatment and medication they thought would help to deal with his bad behaviour. He was diagnosed with many disorders including, *ADD, ADHD, hyper-tension, Tourette's syndrome, Obsessive-Compulsive Disorder* and *Autism*. The list of ailments was endless and none of the various medications he was ever put on improved his behaviour. The psychiatrists all pointed to Seth as troubled from losing his father to suicide and thought that with the proper diagnosis and treatment along with therapy for his behaviour; he might lead a normal life. The real problem in my estimation was that none of these doctors ever got it right.

I tried to give Maria the support that she desperately needed in her battles with Seth and tried to get together with her as much as possible to ease her agony but my children were constant targets of his aggressive behaviour. Even after Maria met Leon Lanix, Seth's behaviour only worsened. Leon had tried to discipline Seth to the best of his abilities but Maria did not let him. She protected Seth to his own detriment. She said to me that the punishments that Leon tried to enforce were too harsh. What she didn't seem to realize and what I noticed was that Seth was winning the battle and had them divided and conquered.

Seth was always totally out of control when he came over to our house and he didn't really seem to know how to behave properly. He liked to pull Jennie's hair and make her cry and he would punch Nick and Peter when they didn`t play games his way.

Seth once attacked Nick for no reason at all when all the cousins were at the beach playing. Nick let all the kids bury him in the sand up to his neck and when they were done, Seth went wild and started jumping all over defenseless Nick. When asked why he did that,

Seth merely said he thought it would be funny to see Nick squirm while he jumped him.

Another time Seth came up from our family room downstairs screaming that he was bitten on his arm by Peter and he showed us teeth marks that were left by Peter. When I went down to our family room to investigate what had happened I found Peter in the corner shaking. Peter yelled that he wasn't sorry for biting Seth because it was the only way he could stop the big beast from choking him. When I looked at Peter's neck, there were red marks left around it from the attack.

"But why did he try to choke you?" I asked.

"I don't know. He all of a sudden went crazy. You should ask that big ball of lard why," shouted Peter.

Seth shouted back, "The little bastard wouldn't trade his *Blastoise Pokemon* card with me, so that's why."

When I heard Seth's explanation, I looked at Doug in such disbelief. Doug angrily told Seth to get out of our house and he said that he was no longer welcome in our home. When Maria heard this she yelled, "Why does Seth always get blamed for everything? Peter's not so fucking innocent himself. Look at the marks he left on Seth's arm?"

"Well those marks are defensive," Doug shouted back. "In a court of law, Peter would be found innocent. I won't tolerate the attacks on our kids anymore."

Maria was angry and grumbled to her kids to get going and she left in a huff and a puff. This seemed to be the turning point in our relationship. For years to come, I still tried to keep in touch with Maria and support her as much as I could but as long as Seth was behaving aggressively, I felt that I had to keep my children at a safe distance from him.

There were more stories about Seth's behaviour that we heard from Emily. She confided in Jennie that she was afraid of her brother, not just because of his sheer size but because he acted so crazy.

Jennie asked Emily to come over for a visit when she heard that she was vividly upset about her brother's behaviour at home. When Emily was over, I heard Jennie say to her, "I know all about craziness Emily. Both my brothers are bi-polar remember?"

"No your brothers are actually nice. They seem to be stable. Seth has stopped taking his medication and he does drugs and he is violent," replied Emily.

I went over to Emily and told her that if she ever felt threatened and needed to stay with us at any time that she was welcome to do so. Emily went on to tell us that Seth not only started smoking pot but he was snorting cocaine and he had tried speed. He had been suspended so many times from high school for his unruly behaviour that the *School Board* had no choice but to finally ban him from all high schools in *London*. He had threatened a principal at school with a chain after the principal had confiscated his drugs and didn't give them back.

"Seth told the principal to fuck himself and then swung the chain at him," said Emily. "The police were called and he is charged with uttering a death threat along with two counts of possession of narcotics. These are serious charges that my Mom has to hire a lawyer now to see if the charges can be lessened and to avoid jail time for Seth."

As I heard all the troubles that Seth was causing, my heart ached for Emily and I felt compelled to call Maria and ask her if there was anything I could do to help.

When I called Maria, she simply said that it was up to Seth to put an effort into changing his ways and improving his life. Leon had enough of his bad behaviour long ago and had given up on ever trying to rehabilitate him. She too was finally sick of it as well and she told me that she didn't think there was anything that could be done with Seth that hadn't been tried already.

"I'm having problems with Emily too," she went on to say. "I came home the other day from work to see the police standing at my doorstep. The first thing I thought of was what did Seth do this time but no it was Emily sitting in the back of the cruiser. She had been caught shoplifting from the mall. She's also been skipping school and smoking pot with some of her friends. It doesn't help her that she's smoking pot while on medication for her anxiety."

All I could think about at that moment was that I had caught Maria stealing from my mother's purse many years ago and this escalated to her stealing from the deli where we worked as well. Now it was her turn to see how it felt to have a daughter for a thief. Instead of rubbing that in her face, I asked her, "Isn't life with teenagers so much fun?"

"I've got two that are useless twits," she said. "They barely know how to tie their own shoes. They both look like they are headed for jail one day and there's very little I can do to stop it."

"You have to stay positive Maria," I replied. "There's always room for improvement."

"Not with these two there isn't," she said. "I'm at my wit's end. I caught Emily having sex in her room the other day and it wasn't with a boy either! She tells me she is bi-sexual you know. I'm not sure what to do with these kids anymore," exclaimed Maria. "My therapist tells me these kids have to stand up and make the changes necessary to improve their own lives and be responsible for their own behaviour. I have done everything in my power to help them over all their troubled years and it has almost cost me my own life. I'm so fucking depressed, I feel like a walking zombie waiting for the right moment to end it all."

When Maria told me this, my heart sank and all I could think of at the moment was to give her a bug hug. Somehow I thought it might help her to gather the strength to carry on in spite of all her frustrations with her children.

"Oh Jeanette, I haven't even told you the worst yet that has happened with Emily lately," said Maria. She sounded so down as she went on to tell me the story. "When Emily was hanging out at the *Medway Arena* close to where we live, I had no idea that she wasn't skating. She had met a guy who works as a security guard at the arena. She told me that he is madly in love with her. He convinced her to go home at lunch time with her and they started having sex on a regular basis."

"How old is he?" I asked Maria.

"Fuck, he's forty-eight years old and she's only fifteen!" exclaimed Maria.

"Holy crap, that's not good," I said to Maria in shock. "What are you going to do?"

"I called the police and they told me that since she is under sixteen, there's no consent and he'll be charged with statutory rape," she said.

"I can't believe that all of this has happened in the short time since we haven't seen much of each other lately Maria. I am really sorry to hear all this and wish there was something I could do to help," I said to her.

"That's okay Jeanette," said Maria. "It's not your fault at all. I know that these kids are my responsibility and as much as I still love them, I really don't hold out much hope for them for the future, especially Seth. There's no paradise here, that's for sure."

I thought to myself that some of the problems Maria was having with these children could be explained by genetics in the fact that Seth and Emily were both born, like their own father was born from alcoholics but this really didn't explain it all. I knew Maria had smoked pot while she was pregnant and it was obvious that this also had an effect on their development. I never discussed this fact with Maria but there was no doubt in my mind that there was still something else wrong, especially with Seth. There was definitely something deadly wrong with him.

CHAPTER TWENTY

Lynn

If my best friend at home was Doug then my best friend at work was Lynn Albright. People can have more than one best friend and I was lucky to have two. She is a very sweet person with a big heart who would help anyone with any problem that they had no matter how big or small.

We went for walks at lunch time together to ward off our frustrations from work and talk about our mundane jobs and vent to each other along the way. We were speed walkers and didn't slow down for anything except for when the bells would chime to a musical tune from the *Dutch* memorial in *Victoria Park*. The memorial was a set of bells that were given by the *Dutch* people as a gift to *Canadians* to remind them of their eternal gratitude for *Canada's* role in the liberation of *Holland*.

As we walked past the bells while they chimed, there was a huge gathering of young people in the park in the middle of the day in April. I wondered what may be going on and Lynn immediately told me that it was the *Kiwanis Music Festival* being held in the park.

"Oh," I said. "I don't hear any music though. It looks like people are playing *Frisbee* while they are waiting for it to start. There's a sweet smell in the air though and I think its pot," I commented.

"Is that what that smell is?" questioned Lynn.

As the receptionist from our office, she kept telling people who came into our office that day, that there was the *Kiwanis Music Festival* going on in the park. Later on that evening while we were on our way home, we had cut through the park and Lynn stopped to ask one of the police officers patrolling what was going on.

"It's four twenty day. April 20th. You know, it's the one day of the year where you can smoke dope in public and we look the other way. We are just here for crowd control purposes," said the officer.

Well, Lynn started to laugh as we found this out. She had been telling people she thought that the gathering was the music festival all day but instead it was a dope fest.

"I told you Lynn," I said to her as I laughed out loud with her. I wonder what's going on this weekend in *Victoria Park*."

"Is it the *Rib Fest?*" asked Lynn. "Or is it the *Kiwanis Music Festival?* I feel like an idiot."

"You're not an idiot Lynn," I said. "You are just so very innocent, that's all. I had a little more experience than you did with dope when I was a teenager. That's the influence of an older brother and twin sister, you know. I'm just glad that my kids don't do drugs and that they are smart enough to stay away from it."

"Me too," said Lynn. "It's harder than ever to keep kids away from drugs these days and now that they are glorifying it with days like this, what is this world coming to?"

Lynn and I were able to talk to each other about many different circumstances that came our way in life and we both tried to make a little difference in the world by helping others as well. Once a month we went after work to the soup kitchen downtown to help serve meals to those less fortunate. It was humbling to help out and realize how lucky that I was to have a job, however mundane and to be able to support my family with the basic necessities of food and shelter. Many of these people were homeless and this was a meal that they appreciated more than I could ever imagine.

There were times when Lynn and I would have some very serious conversations about life. She said to me that if you gathered ten people in a room and asked each of them to place their troubles on the table and then go around and ask each person to pick from the pile, once you saw what troubles were laid out on that table, you would gladly take back your own troubles.

When I thought about it, she was so right. As much as we had struggled with Doug's cancer; there were others, like the mother of Peter's friend at school who had died from breast cancer at age forty-two who was worse off than ourselves. Even though our children had each been afflicted with an illness, at least they were treatable illnesses. I knew of one boy who went to Nick's high school who at age seventeen had hung himself at the playground at his school due to the non-treatment of his mental illness. Another friend of Doug's had recently lost his twenty-six year old son to diabetes. What about poor little Megan Walker down the street who died from complications of appendicitis at age eight? *Gladly, I would keep all of my own troubles and not trade my sorrows,* I thought.

I told Lynn one day that it was interesting how I didn't realize until I reached my forties that I had a mild case of dyslexia. It wasn't ever really a big deal but no wonder that I often got things backwards and it made sense that I didn't like to read when I was growing up. I had to force myself to concentrate extra hard when I went to University and I remember how that five hundred page history book was a challenge for me to read but I persevered and read the whole book.

When I told Lynn about my neighbour who had been in a car accident and was charged with an IUD, she laughed and asked, "Did she get pregnant? Don't you mean charged with a DUI? Drinking Under the Influence?"

It was a bit embarrassing but Lynn never made me feel bad about anything. We had a good laugh! Peter on the other hand was the one who liked to joke about my dyslexia the most. "I bet I know what your favourite number is Mom? Eleven!" he exclaimed.

I went on to explain to Lynn that my dyslexia actually did work in my favour one time when I worked for the President of a land development company. My boss was away on a trip in *Australia* and he had forgotten his scuba diving certificate and couldn't dive without it. He said he tried to call the training centre where he took the course to get a copy but they had no record of it. When he asked me to investigate further, it seemed odd to me that they had a record of him taking the course but not of the actual certificate itself. The certificates were all filed by date of birth. He was born on 02.07.1971. It dawned on me that because I often got numbers backwards, I thought to ask them to check 07.02.1971 and sure enough it popped up. My boss was so elated that he was able to experience the dive at the *Great Barrier Reef* and told me that I had saved the day. I was glad that for once my dyslexia turned out to be advantageous instead of a burden

Lynn and I shared our joys with each other which happened mostly to be about family. Whenever she found a dime on the sidewalk while we were walking, she said that her mother in heaven was thinking about her. She said she missed her mother as I did too, even though she was a grown woman and a mother as well. She never liked anyone wasting her time with playing silly mind games. She would repeat what her mother used to say to her, "If you waste my time, you waste my life."

"You're right about that Lynn," I replied. "Life is too precious to waste, that's for sure."

When Lynn came over to my house for a visit, we talked freely about our everyday experiences involving the kids. I was complaining to her that I was having a hard time getting Peter to take a shower now that he was in grade eight. Since she had three boys that were older, she confidently said, "You just wait. He's at that awkward age right now but once he discovers girls, then you'll be banging on the bathroom door for him to get out of the shower."

Sure enough, the day arrived, not too far off when Peter started jumping in the shower on his own, not once but twice in a day. He had indeed discovered the fact that girls didn't like stinky boys. Lynn had been through it all with her boys and she always had good advice for me.

Ironically, Lynn and I both married a Doug, not the same one that is, that left home at a young age but not for the same reason. Her Doug had left at age sixteen to get away from the religious cult of the *Lutheran Brethren Church*. Their strict doctrine didn't allow the modern world to influence their members so there was no television, no music, no dancing and of course, in later years, no internet. Technology, it was believed was the work of the devil and these were his tools to spread his evil.

Lynn's Doug had made his escape from the church and was immediately ex-communicated along with three of his other older brothers and one sister who had left before him. Out of seven children in his family, only two remained in the Church and remained part of the family. All communication between those that belonged and those that did not ended. Lynn told me that Doug was sad to leave his parents and his younger brother and sister behind but it was a personal choice that everyone had to make for themselves. He told Lynn that he could never understand how anyone could live so restricted by a religion and accept this as God's will.

"God wouldn't want families not to speak to each other. What does that promote?" she asked. "Any religion that cuts you off for questioning their beliefs must be a cult. Doug's family was all brain-washed from a young age to believe that the world was an evil place. There is some truth to that but there is also good in the world so why not embrace the positive instead of the negative and make a change in the right direction. I believe that if you can't change a situation, change the way you feel about it."

"That reminds me about my Doug's past and how he left at age sixteen to escape the physical abuse that his father inflicted on his family," I said to Lynn. "Both of our husbands were boys at the time they were set free from the torment. I think they have turned into appreciative men and are good husbands today now that they are truly leading better lives."

Lynn agreed and said that sometimes her Doug's past would come back to haunt him. He didn't always know how to act in times of trouble. When Lynn had been diagnosed with melanoma two years earlier, he wasn't sure how to support her. She was someone that truly understood what a patient of cancer lives through and how the dreadful disease affects your loved ones.

"Jeanette, I think as hard as it is for the patient themselves going through treatment with the nausea, pain and sickness, it's harder on your loved ones looking back at you. Believe me, I know first-hand that seeing those eyes helplessly looking back hurts," she said.

"You are right. It is difficult when you feel that you can't do anything more to take their pain away and simply try to make them feel more comfortable. When you see the pain in their eyes, you want to magically take it away but you can't," I said.

"My Doug didn't always know what to do when he heard me throwing up in the toilet," she said. "He couldn't handle all the sickness and I could feel his anguish. Even though I was the one who had cancer, we were both battling it."

"Doug said to me that he thought I would run for the hills after he was sick. He said he thought that I wouldn't be able to take all the sickness," I said to her. "I merely told him that he didn't really know me at all then, if he was worried that I would leave. I think he had trouble believing that anyone would stick with him through the hard times because no-one had ever shown him true love before in his life."

"I came over to tell you some bad news Jeanette," said Lynn. "My Doug has lost his job, his benefits and his pension. The company that he managed for twenty-six years was sold to new owners who made some changes and ran the company into the ground in less than two years."

"That's a shame," I said to Lynn. "What is Doug going to do now?"

"Well, he has some loyal clients that still want him to supply them with parts they need for their machinery. He wants to go into business for himself," explained Lynn.

"That's tough, especially in the first year when you have to set your business up and try to get things running smoothly," I replied.

"I told Doug that I would support him in this choice but that if he wasn't making at least ten bucks an hour after the first year, then I wanted him to get a real job that he hates just like the rest of us," she said. "He wants me to cut back on the grocery bill by ten percent though and cut out going to the dentist and getting my hair done."

"Wow, that seems a little drastic but drastic times call for drastic measures," I said.

"Well, I don't mind cutting back on food or the dentist but I told Doug that I would rather give up sex than have to give up getting my hair dyed," Lynn chuckled.

"I don't blame you Lynn," I said. "What is he giving up?" I asked.

"Not a whole lot so I don't know why I have to compromise and he doesn't," she confessed.

"Well, I think he is probably a little worried about your future since all his hard work into the company seemed to be all for nothing," I said. "That can't be a good feeling."

"I know," said Lynn. "I wish we were living under different circumstances though."

"I think you'll get by alright. It'll be a tough first year but give it the time it needs for the business to grow," I said.

From that day forward for a whole year, I asked Lynn every now and again if Doug was making more than ten bucks an hour yet.

"No not yet. Still waiting," she replied.

CHAPTER TWENTY-ONE

Turning Fifty

Who ever said turning fifty was nifty? I asked myself as the big day was approaching for me. I didn't like it one bit. I was turning *fucking fifty* as my sister so delicately put it when I spoke with her about our pending birthday that was coming up in four days. I told Maria that I was not happy with turning into this old lady. When I turned thirty I still felt young. When I turned forty, I suddenly no longer felt young any more but I also didn't feel that old yet and now that I was turning fifty, I started to feel older and I started to look it too. A few more wrinkles, some more grey hair and a few extra pounds.

Ugh, I thought to myself. *It's no fun getting old.* That's what my Dad used to say about getting older as you started to feel all the aches and pains more vividly after turning fifty. My Mom, however, always said, "There really isn't much you can do to change the fact that you are getting older, so make the best use of your time."

The words from the song *Time* by *Pink Floyd* sang in my head, " . . . *ticking away, the moments of a dull day, shorter of breath and one day closer to death.*" How true that time does tick away for all of us, from one generation to the next and every day that we get older brings us one day closer to death.

As Peter put it, "It's the circle of life Mom," as he held our cat *Meowser* up above his head making reference to *Simba* in the *Lion King* movie.

"Thanks Peter," I groaned. "Wait until you get older. I know it's hard to believe that you'll be as old as me one day but your turn is coming sooner than you think."

My fiftieth birthday came with fifty of everything it seemed. Fifty flamingos on the front lawn with a bright neon sign that read *2 SEXY 2B 50*, fifty balloons, fifty candles and not to mention fifty kisses! So a new decade started and I wanted to make sure that this decade wasn't dull and I was going to try harder to get into shape and not be shorter of breath or any closer to death if I could help it. I knew I had to keep active and stay in shape in order to stay healthy. Doug and I both did a lot of walking, biking and hiking in the great outdoors. It was good for the body and a great way to relieve stress in the fast paced world in which we lived.

"We'll just have to do more horizontal aerobics in bed," Doug said about getting into shape. "That's my favourite exercise and the best way of relieving stress."

When I woke up in the middle of the night with night sweats, I said to Doug, "It's no fun going through menopause."

Doug replied, "Oh, menopause, *men and their paws*. Come closer and I'll show you what my paws can do to make you feel better." I chuckled as his gentle caresses made my skin tingle and made me feel good all over.

I felt fortunate that I made it to fifty without any major health problems and that I had never broken any bones in my body. I was only ever admitted to the hospital three times in my life and each time it was to have a baby. Now for Doug, he had been in and out of the hospital so many times that he had used up eight of his nine lives by the time he reached fifty. I called him *Sylvester* and told him that he had better be careful not to use up the last life that he had left.

Then the day arrived that I dreaded from the moment Doug had bought a motorcycle. He bought a fancy highway cruising bike that had a seat on it with a backrest for me. Doug said to me that he wasn't sure at first if I would like the bike. I told him that I had ridden on my brother's motorcycle when I was a kid and thought it was thrilling. I also told him that a friend of mine had become a quadriplegic when she was thrown from the bike that her boyfriend was driving many years ago.

"They aren't called death machines for nothing," I said to him.

"Quit worrying and hop on," Doug said. "Let's go motorcycle-mama." Then I knew it was time to hit the open road. I thought that there were risks in life whether you drove in a car or flew in an airplane or simply crossed the road running to catch the bus. If it was your time to go I really didn't think there was much you could do to stop it. On the other hand, there was no reason to act recklessly either.

I put the negative thoughts out of my mind and enjoyed the rides that we often took and ended up in nearby *Komoka* or *Coldstream* conservation areas and hiked whenever the weather was good. On the way back, we stopped at the local coffee shop and sat outside and met up with the other bikers in the parking lot. They too stopped in for coffee and it seemed funny to me how there seemed to be a common connection with these people simply because we rode a motorcycle. Bikers waved to us with two fingers at the side as we travelled along the road and passed each other going in opposite directions. It was a common etiquette that meant peace and safe travel.

We met a couple who each rode their own *Harley Davidson* motorcycles. The man Brian Davies was tall, burly looking with little hair and had tattoos all over his arms. His wife Carolyn Davies was short, a little on the chunky side, wore all leather and had a small salamander tattoo on her left index finger. They seemed like a well suited couple and other than their somewhat gruff exterior;

they seemed like a very normal couple to me. Brian told us that he worked as a welder and Carolyn worked in a music store in the mall. They talked about their two children, Rick, the oldest son who was twenty and was off to college while their youngest daughter Chelsey was only eleven but acted like she was sixteen.

Doug and I both looked at each other and spoke out loud at the same time, "That sounds familiar."

I went on to tell them about our children, our oldest son Nick who also was at college and our youngest Jennie who was thirteen going on eighteen. I said that we just had that middle child Peter in between to contend with. They laughed and said that's why they never had a middle child because if they had, then they would have been out numbered.

They went on to tell us about the trip that they took last summer on their bikes to *Montreal*. Chelsey had gone with them and enjoyed it thoroughly. They all planned to travel again on their bikes out west to visit *Banff National Park* this summer. It was a carefree life and an easy way to travel. Doug and I had talked about possibly doing that some day but instead of taking our bike, I said that I wanted to travel with the truck and trailer back out west. Although it appealed to me to travel lighter and more carefree on the bike, I enjoyed the thoughts of bringing the luxuries and comforts of our trailer with us.

As we watched them leave, I pointed out to Doug that there was a sticker on Brian's bike that read, *do you believe in Life after Death? FUCK with my bike and you'll find out!* Doug and I both started to laugh as we waved goodbye to them.

"Is it mostly a lower class of people who ride motorcycles?" I asked Doug.

"There are all kinds, of course," he said. "We have met all types of people from all walks of life who enjoy the ride. You can't simply judge someone to have class just by whether they ride a motorcycle or not."

"I agree with you. That reminds me of the time that Richard had asked me if you were *cultured* after I first met you, remember?" I asked.

"Well, what did you say to him?" asked Doug.

"I told him it was none of his business. Just because you were a truck driver, he thought you were at a lower class than him. I told him that you had more class in your baby finger than he'll ever have in his whole body."

Doug wasn't cultured the way Richard said he should be but he was a good man who treated me well and didn't fool around on me. We were always together and enjoyed many activities in life, like camping, riding our motorcycle and going on hikes. Richard could take all his culture and stuff it as far as I was concerned. It wasn't about the types of things that a person did that made them cultured but it was a sense of self-worth and how they treated others that counted most. Richard always put on an heir of being cultured but he ended up acting like a selfish fool instead.

While I enjoyed going to the theatre with Richard and playing tennis and going golfing with him when we had first met so long ago, I enjoyed my new life with Doug so much more no matter what it was that we did. Our motorcycle rides were fun and it kept us close, especially when I literally clutched onto to him for dear life when he took off down the road. Doug was a safe driver but it was all those bad drivers not paying attention to the motorcyclists on the road that were a hazard.

Now, I knew this day would arrive when he stared death in the face from that motorcycle. He had been out on his motorcycle touring the back roads on a beautiful day as the sun was going down. He was an experienced rider and the roads were good but it had been unavoidable. A deer had jumped out of nowhere in front of his bike and he ended up in the ditch. He was in pretty bad shape when I went to go and see him in the hospital that day. When I arrived, the doctors reassured me that although he was all bandaged up, he was going to survive.

The first thing I said to him when I saw him was, "Now you've got yourself in a real pickle *Sylvester*. What am I going to do with you? Haven't you had enough of pain and hospitals for one lifetime? My vows were for in sickness and in health. I'm kind of sick of the sickness part and want more of the health part if you can imagine that?"

"I know. I've put you through hell over the last decade but I'm still hopelessly in love with you after all these years. Doesn't that count for something?" he pleaded.

"I guess so but you've used up all of your nine lives," I said as I tried to give him a kiss somewhere but there was no spot left that wasn't all bandaged up. "Can you promise me that you'll stay out of the hospital for at least the next ten years?" I pleaded. "After all we've been through together; I want to make it to retirement with you in one piece."

CHAPTER TWENTY-TWO

Misery

Maria was home making a cup of tea when she received the call from the police sergeant at the *London Middlesex Detention Centre.* She called me right after to tell me that her son had been arrested once again and was being held at the *Centre.*

"When the police called," she said to me, "I felt a shudder go through my body and watched as the hair on my arms stood straight up. I've been called by the police on many occasions before but somehow I felt that this time it was different."

Seth had been arrested on other occasions and was charged with possessing drugs and uttering a death threat when he was still a juvenile and his record had been erased. Since then, he was in and out of jail for the same types of charges but now he would be tried as an adult.

"I don't even want to go see him in jail this time," said Maria. "He won't ever change."

"You don't know that for sure," I said to Maria. I wondered what Seth had been charged with this time.

Seth had grown to be a burly guy by the time he reached eighteen. He stood six foot tall, was two hundred and fifty pounds and had a foot size of fifteen. He was a massive guy and to see him with his dark curly hair and hollow-looking eyes, you would look the other way and mind your own business if you met him on the street.

Maria had explained to me that he was the right size to play football and he actually played for his first two years of high school but then he quit the team in the middle of grade eleven. His sheer size made it impossible for him to keep up to the physical demands of the practices and games. Maria had been happy at first when he tried out and made the junior football team because it gave him a purpose to go to school along with an outlet for his aggression. The coach liked his size and tried to shape Seth into a real football player and thought that he had the potential to become a good player but Seth was too out of shape to keep up and didn't have the right attitude either.

"He always wanted to kill the other team and bust their balls," said Maria.

"That's not really smart is it?" I questioned.

"His coach had pulled Seth aside and explained to him that a good football player is a smart football player. The game was one of mental strategy as much as a physical one. It wasn't about going out to bust heads but it was a game of skill," said Maria.

"Seth doesn't seem to really understand how a real athlete plays the game does he? It sounds like he is too aggressive and brutal in his approach to the game in the way he acts off the field as well," I said to Maria.

"After he quit the team, he also stopped going to school and started to spiral downward from there. When he started experimenting with drugs and alcohol, there was no stopping him on this deadly road of destruction," she said. "After all I've been through in my life so far; nothing prepared me for what has happened now. Seth has been arrested for first degree murder."

When she told me this, the word murder repeated in my mind, over and over. I knew her son had many issues but I never would have thought that he was capable of this. *How did he turn into this monster?* I questioned myself. I always thought that Maria had tried her best with him and gave him so many chances in life to try to makes things better for himself. She confessed to me that she felt that she had failed completely in keeping him from committing such a hideous crime.

"You can't blame yourself for his actions Maria," I said to her.

"That's easy for you to say, he's not your fucked up son," she said sadly to me.

When Maria went to the trial to hear the details of the case, she told me that she could no longer stand to be there. The jury was told how Seth and his girlfriend had had a fight the night of the murder. They were arguing with each other and this escalated into his girlfriend hitting him with a plastic baseball bat. This infuriated Seth and made him go to the garage and grab a real bat and come after her with a fury that didn't stop until, "All the blood oozed out of her head."

Seth confessed on the stand that he tried to clean up the blood to make the scene look less horrifying but there was too much blood soaked into the couch and floor. He said that he panicked and fled the house on foot and stayed in hiding until he was caught by the police two weeks later. At first he had pleaded not guilty to the charges by reason of insanity but he was found unanimously guilty by the jury after only two hours of deliberations. His sentence was for life in a maximum security prison in *Kingston, Ontario* with no chance of parole for twenty-five years.

"My heart is broken but ironically, I feel that a weight has been lifted now that I know that Seth will not hurt anyone for at least the next quarter century," said Maria. "I can finally move on now with my life with Leon and Emily but I wonder if it is all too late."

"Let's hope it isn't too late," I said to Maria.

CHAPTER TWENTY-THREE

Temper Control

Although Doug was strong and rugged with handsome looks on the outside, I noticed that he had another side to him that was fragile at times on the inside. There was a reason Doug took *Tai Kwan Do* when he was seventeen. He told me that after he left home when he was sixteen, he had a rage inside that he recognized in himself that needed to be kept under control, so he learnt the finer art of discipline through the fine art of combat. Learning the techniques of this martial art seemed to help Doug tremendously with controlling his outbursts that he had locked up inside from his childhood.

Before we were married, Doug's mother had warned me that although he had always been a good kid when he grew up, he had a hard time dealing with stress and thought I would have my hands full with him. I thought that we had a great relationship, so I wasn't quite sure what she meant by her analysis, but over time it became a little clearer.

Throughout our marriage, I witnessed various times when Doug snapped as he became angry. The first time was early on in our marriage when we had finished painting the outside of our house. Once he was finished painting, Doug took the extra paint from the can and dumped the extra paint in the catch basin at the road in the front of our house.

When I asked him, "What are you doing? You're staining the curb blue!" I went on to ask, "How can you be so stupid?"

"Well, that's easy for me. Maybe next time, you can fucking paint the whole house by yourself," shouted Doug as he stomped away.

I stood there not realizing what I had said to make him explode like that. It was the first time I had heard him swear like that and I felt horrible when I came to realize that I had called him stupid. I looked at the curb stained with blue paint and went inside shaking my head. It wasn't until later that night when Doug had calmed down enough for me to apologize to him that I learnt something about the word stupid. It had been a word that his father had repeated to him over and over as he grew up.

"You're so stupid. You'll never amount to anything. That's what my father told me over and over," said Doug. "It was one word that triggered a rage in me, so please don't ever use that word around me."

I knew then, not to ever use that word again in front of him.

Doug could not take criticism at all either. I had to be careful what I said to him when it came to work that he did around the house. I commented that the caulking job that he did in the bathroom didn't look right to me. It was bubbled and I asked if he could fix it. He gave me a look that made me shudder and threw the pliers into the floor with all his force. I was too shocked to say anything to him after that while he was in that state of mind. Later on that evening, I told him that I was frightened by his anger.

He apologized to me and said that he would never hurt me but he was frustrated by what I said to him. He explained to me that by questioning his abilities, it was just like his father used to do and this triggered the rage inside that he could not easily control. At this point, I was starting to see what his mother meant by having my hands full with him.

There was another time when the motor from our boat was stolen from our driveway just a couple of days before we were going to leave on vacation. I had never seen Doug so enraged by what happened. When I came home he was in our room, lying in bed starring off into space. I noticed that he was red in the face and looked very furious.

Since it was only a motor that got stolen, I tried to make light of the situation thinking that and it wasn't the end of the world and said to him, "It's not a big deal. We can replace the motor through our insurance, don't worry about it." He didn't say a word but just got up out of bed and punched the first thing that was in his way. I felt lucky that it wasn't me but instead he had punched the fan in our bedroom into a hundred pieces.

Later once Doug could see straight again, he explained that he couldn't stand people who stole things from others. It infuriated him because once in his childhood years he had his hard-earned money stolen from him. Doug had worked since he was eleven in the tobacco field for five seasons. He was told by his parents that he had to put his earnings in the bank and that he could only spend a small portion and the rest was going to be kept for him for the future. After five years when Doug finally said to his father that he wanted to have his money to buy a motor-cross bike, most of the money from his account was gone.

"When I asked my father what happened to all my money, he just asked me, *what do you think happened to all the money? Do you think you would get away with not paying room and board all these years?* I was devastated when he told me this Jeanette," said Doug.

"That is awful Doug. What did your mother say about all this?" I asked.

"She didn't say much and agreed with him that as the father of the household he had a right to the money," he told me.

"Oh Doug, that's shameful on both their parts. Who takes money from their own child at age eleven for room and board? Only a drunken idiot would do that," I exclaimed.

"It still makes my blood boil to this day when I think back to that day," Doug recalled. "He stole that money just to support a lousy stinking booze habit. Now you understand a bit better why I don't like boozers or crooks and he was both."

"I understand completely and see that when the boat motor got stolen, it triggered these bad memories for you. Will you ever be able to get over this?" I questioned.

"I don't know Jeanette. I really wish that my past didn't haunt me so much. I have come a long way by talking to you about all of this and trying to deal with all this pent up anger and frustration," he confessed. "I really don't mean to take things out on you and I would certainly never hurt you. You have helped me with so much in life, I can't begin to tell you how much I love and appreciate you."

"Thanks Doug. That's more than Richard ever did, that's for sure," I said. "After he left me, he told me that he hoped one day that I would meet someone who appreciated me and so you will have to thank him for that!"

"I did that once already, remember? I shook his hand and thanked him for screwing up his marriage," said Doug. "The look on his face at the time was priceless."

"You crack me up Doug and that's why I love you," I said.

I did love Doug very much but there was a time when his temper scarred me the most the day he stepped in cat poop down on the floor in his work shop. He came up from down stairs and yelled, "That's the last time that cat is going to poop outside the box!" We all snickered and thought he was making a joke but he was livid.

"Where's that cat?" he asked. "He's going to be a dead cat when I catch him!" he screamed. The kids went running when they heard how upset Doug really was. Doug grabbed the cat carrier and went into Jennie's room where the kids were trying to hide the cat and he said in a very stern voice to them, "Give me that cat now."

By this time the kids were crying but stopped immediately when Doug yelled, "Now!"

I wasn't sure what to say or do but I knew that I had to say something to Doug to make him stop. "Doug, what are you going to do with the cat?" I asked.

He looked me straight in the eye and said, "I won't kill him myself but I'm taking him to the vet to be euthanized. I'm sick and tired of that cat pooping on my floor." Then he turned to the kids and said, "One of us has got to go. It's either me or the cat!" he said in a very serious tone.

I immediately thought that this was one of those types of questions that should never be asked let alone answered. It was an unfair question and one that once asked and answered, couldn't be taken back. The kids loved their Dad even if he had been very difficult to live with lately but they loved their cat too. I was sure that what the kids were going to say next would push Doug over the edge.

I knew he had been feeling depressed lately due to complications from the surgery five months earlier. He couldn't eat much with only one third of his stomach left and his digestive system still wasn't working properly. He was constantly fighting hard to stabilize his weight so that he could return to work and try to feel normal again. It was all about normalcy. *How do you ever get back to normal after cancer, after treatments, after surgery,* I questioned myself. It had been a long year and a half journey since that first day that we found out Doug had cancer. The shrinking of the tumour, the surgery, the weight loss and now the post surgery complications had all cumulated and had come to a head. Our family doctor was right when she had predicted a long road for Doug. *But where was this road leading?* I asked myself.

"You can go, not Meowser," they shouted. I knew then that was the answer I dreaded that they would say. Doug looked infuriated.

I tried to reason with Doug and asked him, "How could you even ask them that question? They love their cat. You can't be serious?"

"Well, I guess they love that cat more than me. They made their choice, I'm leaving," said Doug. He went to pack a bag with some clothes and grabbed his pills and walked right out the front door as we all watched in disdain.

"He'll be back home Mom," said Peter. Peter must have seen the look of horror on my face when Doug left. He didn't seem worried but Jennie started crying.

"I'm not so sure about that Peter," I replied. "Dad has been very depressed lately since his operation and you know how that feels. I'm worried."

Nicholas looked worried too. He said that he had noticed a change in Doug's attitude since surgery. I thought that it hadn't been easy for any of us coping with the recovery from surgery.

"Mom, I've never seen him so angry and all about that stupid cat," said Nick. Nick turned to Peter and Jennie and said to them, "Why didn't you guys just agree to put that dumb cat out of his misery and do us all a favour."

"No. Daddy has been yelling at us a lot lately about everything. How could he think of killing Meowser? I'm glad he's gone. He hasn't been nice to you lately either Mom. You have done so much for him. You shouldn't have to take that crap at all," she insisted.

"Instead, Dad stepped in the crap," said Peter as he laughed.

"Now, listen up everyone," I started to say. "Dad's been under a lot of stress lately. He's not been feeling well so naturally he will be short tempered. He's been through so much agony since surgery and how would you like to walk in his shoes for a day?"

"You're right Mom," said Peter. "That's a point well taken."

"When is he ever going to feel better Mom?" asked Jennie.

"Let's hope soon. In the meantime, I need all of your help to make this work," I replied. "Dad needs us all more than ever right now."

After a couple of hours, I called Doug on his cell phone and asked him how he was doing.

"Can you meet me in the *Superstore* parking lot? I'm not far from home and I'm feeling lousy," he replied. I could tell that he possibly meant that he was feeling guilty about his actions. When I met Doug in the parking lot, I jumped in his truck and asked him what was really going on.

"I think everyone is better off without me," he said. "I've been putting you and the kids through hell and it hurts. I don't want to hurt you or them anymore."

"Well, yes, it's been a little rocky lately but it's not anything we can't handle," I said softly. "I think you need help Doug. More help than we can give you. Maybe some anti-depressants will help." I hoped that he wouldn't get angry with me for suggesting this to him. He said nothing so I went on to say, "Please for your sake and all of ours, promise me you'll go to the doctor. I need my old jovial Doug back. I miss him."

That's when Doug put his head into his hands and started to sob. I pulled him close and told him it was alright and that things will get better.

Finally, Doug stopped crying and said, "I was tempted to take all these pills Jeanette but I couldn't do it. When the kids chose the cat over me it made me feel worthless but I realize that it was unfair of me to put them in that position. My family is very important to me and I didn't fight hard all this time to just give up now. Do you forgive me?"

"Yes, I sure do Doug," I said. "Let's go home."

"What will the kids say?" he asked.

"Nothing," I replied. "They understand how you've been feeling lately and they are very resilient. Just don't take their cat away from them."

"I realize that I have an internal struggle that I don't have to face alone," said Doug. "I'm glad that I can share my pain with my family and I know that you will all be there for me. I'm not going to let cancer or any of the aftermaths ruin my family. I promise I'll make that appointment tomorrow Jeanette."

CHAPTER TWENTY-FOUR

Aaron

My brother Mark came to visit us at *Algonquin Park* the following summer with his daughter Laura. Mark's wife had just started a new job and didn't have any vacation time coming to her, so he came to camp just with the two of them.

On the first day, we went hiking on the *Beaver Pond Trail* and saw lots of wildlife. There were beautiful blue herons in the marshy area and a great big bull moose proudly displaying his rack of horns. We all knew to stay back and observe the wildlife and appreciate it from a distance. Some people had no respect for wildlife though and risked encounters.

I was telling Mark that one day, there was a moose that wandered into *Rock Lake* camp one early morning and people went running towards it to take pictures of this magnificent animal. They spooked the moose and luckily it trotted away instead of rushing them.

"I can't believe how dumb some people can be," said Mark. "It's never a smart move to approach a moose like that."

"They were lucky that it wasn't rut season," said Doug. "If that was the case, it's like a train wreck waiting to happen. In fact, they'd look like ground up hamburger when the moose was done with them."

"Another time, we saw people up on the ledge here in camp taking pictures of some cute bear cubs," I said to Mark. "What they didn't realize is that they were in the path of Mama Bear who was coming up from behind them. I never saw people run so fast in all my life. They could have been bear meat if they had gotten any closer to those cubs."

"It's too bad that people can't respect these animals and watch from a safe distance," said Mark.

"Most fatal encounters with wild animals are the fault of dumb-asses like those people," said Doug.

Before dinner time, the kids went off to fish from the old train bridge that was abandoned by the railway. I asked Mark why Aaron, Mark's oldest son who was seventeen years old now had not come camping with them.

"Did he not want to be away from his girlfriend?" I asked.

"No, his relationship with her is over. After four years, I think she has finally had enough of his erratic behaviour," Mark replied.

"Wow, they went out for a long time," I said. "What happened?"

"Well, it's a long story but Aaron has been acting wild for quite some time now. His marks have dropped in school and he is constantly butting heads with his Mom," said Mark. "We can't really leave him home alone or else the house is in ruins when we get back."

"That sounds just like you Mark when you were that age, remember?" I retorted. "You were known as *Mr. Partier* with all your friends when Mom and Dad left on their vacations to *Florida*."

"This is completely different," said Mark. "We partied alright but we never wrecked the house while doing it. Aaron and his so called friends actually trashed the house while we were away and he didn't clean up or try to fix anything. He had over a hundred kids in the house and they all drank and smoked and he didn't stop any of them from going crazy and wrecking the furniture among other things. It was a disaster when we got home and Aaron didn't seem to care at all."

"That's a little different Mark," said Doug. "Did he learn his lesson?"

"Nope," replied Mark. "We tried to ground him but he just laughed at us."

"I wouldn't put up with that crap," Doug said to Mark. "If Nick or Peter ever tried to act like that, their ass would be in a sling."

"Actually, that wasn't even the worst of it," Mark went on to say. "Aaron has been using drugs too and skipping school and acting strangely. He has also been threatening his little sister if she snitches on him about anything. He said he would kill her if she told us about him skipping school and taking drugs."

"That doesn't sound good at all Mark," I said sympathetically. "Have you taken him to a doctor?"

"Yes, we've taken him to a bunch of different doctors and specialists. Aaron was not getting up out of bed to go to school and was constantly complaining about stomach pains. None of the tests showed that there was anything physically wrong with Aaron," said Mark.

"What about his soccer?" I asked. "Does he still play competitively?"

"He lost interest in playing but he has started to body build," replied Mark. "I'm a little afraid of him with those muscles he has now and what he may be capable of doing. He's really strong. One day he got so mad while he was in the car while his girlfriend was driving that he punched the windshield and it smashed into smithereens."

"Wow. That sounds scary Mark," I commented. "He could have killed the two of them."

"Yes, it scared his girlfriend and she wanted to break-up with him but he begged her not to leave. He is always looking at himself in the mirror and talking about how great he is in front of her. She finally had enough of his stupid behaviour and she dumped him," said Mark.

"She seemed like a nice girl when we met her last year," I commented.

"She is a very nice girl. We took her along with us on a vacation to *Disney World* this past February and we all had a great week until the last day. Our plane was delayed due to a storm so we had to depart the plane. Aaron wasn't happy to do so and when he started to descend the stairway, he yelled out, *you fuckers! How dare you delay our flight?* He wasn't even joking. He was serious!" explained Mark.

"Wow, that sounds very peculiar," I remarked. "Did you ever think he might have something mentally wrong with him Mark?" I questioned. "There is a fine line that is referred to as normal behaviour and with teenagers, this range is a little wider than for the rest of us but there is a limit. We all tend to be depressed at times, about things that happen in life and that's normal but a person with an illness like bi-polar disorder has a deep depression that lasts for weeks at a time. Conversely, they may go for weeks where they act grandiose and feel larger than life and then there are periods of relative normalcy in between. Have you seen any signs of this in Aaron at all?"

"Yes, he has been down for weeks at a time and then he seems fine for a while. We thought that he might be bi-polar or at least be suffering from depression but Aaron categorically denies that there is anything wrong with him," said Mark. "We made an appointment with a psychiatrist but he won't go. How did you get Nick to admit that he was bi-polar?"

"Well, that is a whole story on its own. Nick was only twelve at the time that we saw the first signs of trouble with him and he actually had shown signs of paranoia too which can be associated with episodes of bi-polar. As you know, he ended up in the hospital on two separate occasions and we had a hard time keeping him on his medication. After he became catatonic the second time, he realized the severity of not taking his medication," I explained.

"It was a hard time for Nick," said Doug. "I think it's harder to accept the older they get. We were fortunate that Nick's bi-polar was diagnosed and treated at a younger age."

"What are you going to do Mark?" I asked.

"I'm not sure what I can do, if Aaron won't admit that there is anything wrong with himself," said Mark sadly.

"Don't give up Mark. Keep a close eye on him and try to convince him that it's nothing to feel ashamed about," I tried to console him. "Bi-polar disorder is an illness that a person can be afflicted with just as any other type of illness whether it's of the mind or body. The drug *Lithium* that both Nick and Peter take is a chemical that has stabilizing effects in the treatment of their moods. It has been tremendous in helping both of them lead normal lives."

"What is *normal* these days?" asked Mark. "It's such a blur. How can you tell?"

When the kids came back from fishing, they showed off several nice lake trout that they caught from the train bridge at *Whitefish Lake*. It was so scenic there on a clear night and peaceful with the call of the loons that echoed off the lake. I didn't know what life was going to bring next for any of us so I thought that it was time to simply enjoy a little piece of paradise while I could at camp.

Around the campfire that night, everyone joked and laughed and I truly savored the moment. Of course, there are always some people who like to spoil things in camp. Although *Rock Lake* had mostly families with some older couples camping, there was the odd group of young people that came to camp to party instead of to enjoy the peace and quiet. This night we encountered such a group. They gathered out at the beach in front of our site. One guy had an acoustic guitar and began to play and sing while others joined in on the song. Ordinarily it wouldn't have posed a problem but they had been drinking and started to get louder and became boisterous.

We heard one girl ask the guy playing on the guitar, "Do you have a girlfriend?"

He replied, "Is that an invitation?"

It's not that this type of talk bothered anyone but we were here to enjoy the otherwise quiet campground. As their voices and tone started to get louder, Mark suggested that we should call the warden to pay them a visit, especially since we knew him so well since it didn't sound like they were going to move on anytime soon.

Before we knew it, Doug said, "Forget that. I'll set them straight," as he got up out of his chair and headed down toward those drunks. In a deep resounding voice we heard him ask, "Hey, do you think you are the only ones here in this camp? We are sitting right over here, trying to enjoy our campfire. Do you think you could either drink a cup of *shut the hell up* or get the hell out of here?"

Suddenly, the music and silliness stopped and one girl replied, "Hey, do you like the *Backstreet Boys*?"

"NO," shouted Doug as his voice carried across the water and all around camp. We all snickered about this back at our campsite. It was funny how the *Backstreet Boys* were popular back in our day and now they were coming back in popularity but obviously not with Doug.

The group grumbled a bit and as they started to leave, one of the girls stated, "Wow, he's an old grump. Why can't he be happy?"

We all laughed as Doug came back to his seat and said, "There you have it. I don't mind people having fun but there's a time and place for everything and this is neither the time nor place for that bullshit."

"I'm with you Doug," said Mark.

"Me too, you old grump," I said. "It's funny how young people think anyone over forty is old. I remember thinking the same way when I was in my twenties."

"Kids these days," stated Doug. "If only they knew that life was not just one big party."

When I looked at Mark, I could tell that he was deep in thought and had a concerned look on his face. I sympathized with Mark and knew firsthand how it felt to watch your child go down a path that was leading to self-destruction. You feel helpless while you can only watch, wait and wonder how it will all turn out.

CHAPTER TWENTY-FIVE

Cruise

For our twentieth wedding anniversary, Doug and I finally went on a canal bus cruise to *Holland*. We had always talked about going on a cruise together some day and the day had finally arrived.

Doug teased me by saying, "So, you want to go on a cruise do you? I'll take you on a cruise alright. How about going on a cruise missile?"

"Ha, ha," I said. "Aren't you a funny guy?"

Well, after all these years, here we were in the *Netherlands* site-seeing and touring the country where my parents had grown up. It conjured up mixed feelings for me to experience the place where my parents had lived through both the good times before the war and the bad times during the *Second World War*. This war had lasted for five long years and my parents were teenagers at the time when the war had broken out.

I told Doug the story of how my mother and her sister Wilma had to ride their bicycles to their uncle's farm out in the country to try to smuggle some food back to the family in the City during the last year of the war. They were only twelve and thirteen years old at the time and there wasn't enough food to eat during the *hunger winter* as they called it. They each brought back a frozen turkey under their dresses and pretended that they were pregnant to fool the German guards. When they arrived back into the city limits of *Amsterdam*, one *Gestapo* guard stopped them to ask where they were going since it was getting dark and no-one was allowed to be out after dark. My mother, who was younger, instantly froze in her tracks while my aunt simply said to the guards in German that she was tired and pregnant and heading home which was just around the corner. She asked him if he wanted a smoke and offered him a pack of cigarettes as she winked at him. She didn't smoke but kept a pack on her at all times to buy her way out of bad situations. The guard let them go but he could easily have just shot them in the street for concealing food. Most German soldiers were ruthless and not known for being compassionate but in this case the young girls were fortunate to have survived the ordeal.

As Doug and I stood in the one hundred and twenty acre urban *Vondlepark* in *Amsterdam*, I thought about how unique this park was in the middle of such a great city. The name of the park literally translated into English as the *fondle park*.

"I remember my Dad telling me that it was a park where a lot of fondling took place by young lovers," I said to Doug. "I wonder if my parents had ever visited this park in their younger days."

There was so much to see and do when we were in *Amsterdam*. We went to see the spectacular *Keukenhof tulip* festival where there were thousands of tulips and other spring flowers all blooming in a vibrant sea of colour over acres of land. There were several parades to watch with concerts, dance performances and great food to enjoy at the festival.

We visited the *Rijksmuseum* in *Amsterdam* and saw painter *Rembrandt van Rijn's* famous painting *De Nachtwacht* meaning, *the night watch*. To see this painting in real life was overwhelming. It's sheer size and beauty up close was anything short of amazing. No pictures were allowed to be taken in the museum to preserve the oils in the painting. It was strictly forbidden because any artificial light could damage the canvas which would allow it to fade.

"The art in this collection is so beautiful Jeanette," said Doug.

"I didn't think a guy like you could be so cultured Doug," I said as I laughed. "It is amazing to see all of this art in person."

We also went to the visit the place where my parents once worked together at a textile factory in *Amsterdam*. It made me think about the day that my parents had first met and had fallen in love and then had left their jobs, friends, parents and other family members behind to start a new life together far away from the Germans. It was hard to imagine the horror that occurred when the Germans occupied the streets of *Amsterdam* so many years back. We now walked freely due to the sacrifice of many others, including Canadian soldiers who gave up their lives for our freedom.

Even though *Amsterdam* is such a vibrant city today, I noticed that it was also a very crowded city. As much as it was a great place to visit to see the historic buildings and heritage, I couldn't wait to go back home again. We lived in such a great country here in *Canada*, free from the fear of oppression. I now better understood the reasons why my parents left *Holland* to live in a land of opportunity that was far away from war-torn *Europe*.

On our last day in *Holland,* as Doug and I enjoyed the little deli markets and shops and all the other tourist areas where the canal bus took us, I suggested that we visit a cousin of mine while we were in *Amsterdam*. I looked up my cousin Sabrina Van Oster from my father's side of the family and we went to visit her. We found out that she had married her high school sweetheart Hank de Nueker and had two children with him.

"He turned out to be a lousy husband," she said to me. "He was loose as a goose. Now I am re-married to Hank Van Oster who is a great guy."

"That's good to hear Sabrina. I made that dumb mistake too of marrying the wrong guy the first time around. How is your brother Ronald doing?" I asked.

"I'm sad to say that he died many years ago," Sabrina told us.

"I'm sorry to hear that Sabrina," I replied. "What happened? He was a barrel of fun as I remembered him when we were kids."

"You only knew the fun side of him but he had a whole other dark side to him that came out in his late teenage years. When he was seventeen, he took his own life. He only left a note that said that he couldn't take the pain any longer," she said sadly.

"That's terrible Sabrina. I never knew about that, I'm so sorry to hear that," I said.

"It was sad but the only good thing that came from his death was that his mental illness made me take note of my own daughter's behaviour," she said. "Niki had been so moody all through her teenage years and she used to stay out all night at parties until one day she stood on a bridge and thought she could fly. It scared me but I think it was a cry for help. After my experience with Ronald's suicide, it made me stop and take note," said Sabrina. "She is doing fine now that she is on medication for bi-polar disorder. She is a creative director in the film industry."

"Luckily, our daughter who is an artist and fashion designer never developed this illness but both of our sons did. We went through hell with them too but they are both doing fine now that they were diagnosed and treated as well. Nick is a web site designer and Pete plays in a metal band touring North America. Bi-polar really does seem to run in the family genes though," I commented to my cousin.

"Yes, it runs in the *jeans*," joked Doug as he pointed to the jeans that he was wearing.

"Yes, my Dad too had quite the mood swings in his day," said Sabrina. "We always had to walk on egg shells around him when we grew up. His mother, our *Oma* also had her moodiness if you remember."

As we flew home, I pondered the state of my extended family's mental health and wondered for how many generations had this illness been passed down and worse yet, for how many generations had the undiagnosed suffering gone on.

When we arrived home, I *googled* the many famous people of today and in history who were bi-polar or who had bouts of manic depression. The list was long and included such names as *Vincent Van Gogh*, the Dutch artist, who cut off his own ear because he heard voices and wanted them to stop; *Ozzy Osbourne*, one of my favourite singers, no wonder he was crazy enough to bite the heads off bats during his concerts; and one of my favourite authors, *Sidney Sheldon*. Many of these people are very artistic and creative despite their bouts of depression; in fact, it was the mania part of their disorder that many believe gave them an edge with their creativity.

When we got back home from our trip, I felt compelled to give Mark a call about getting his son Aaron the help he needed before it was too late. I phoned Mark and asked him how Aaron was doing.

"Not great," he replied. "He left home a couple of weeks ago and I haven't heard from him since. It isn't unusual for him to leave for a few days at a time but it's been weeks now and I'm definitely worried."

I told Mark about the visit that we had with our cousin Sabrina and her daughter Niki's experience with bi-polar disorder and her own brother's suicide. He was quite shocked to hear the news about our Cousin Ronald's death in the way that it occurred and at such a young age.

"Now if we count up all those in the family who have some kind of mood disorder, there's at least nine. Dad, Maria, Matt, Nick, Peter, Sabrina's daughter Niki, our cousin Ronald, our Uncle Joep and Oma Celia," I pointed out. "There have been so many famous people with the disorder as well, so this illness doesn't discriminate. You have to get through to Aaron before it's too late."

"I'm hoping he'll be alright but it's out of my hands," he said sadly. "He's twenty-one now and he's old enough to make his own decisions."

"The real problem though Mark, is that if he's in a mania state of mind, he won't make the right decisions for himself," I replied. "Bi-polar patients often have poor judgment and make poor choices in life as you know. Look at Matt, for example. After thirty-one years of marriage, he leaves his wife and four children for a broad thirteen years younger. What do you call that behaviour?"

"That's erratic behaviour. It doesn't fucking make sense to me at all Jeanette," Mark replied. "His wife Mary was always good to him I thought but you really don't know what's going on in someone else's head."

"Matt admitted to me that he was depressed for the last five years of his marriage but he never went to the doctor for help," I told Mark. "He said he fell out of love in his marriage and now that he has found love again, he's not depressed anymore."

"He needs more than a younger broad to help him with that," said Mark. "Good luck to him. I have my own worries."

I told Mark that I too was worried about Aaron and it scared me to think that he was out on the streets somewhere without contact with his family in a frame of mind that was less than ideal.

"Don't worry so much Jeanette," said Mark. "I'm going to look for him and try to get him to come back home. Thanks for all your concern."

When Mark hung up the phone, I had a sinking feeling in the pit of my stomach. I hated those feelings that I got but this time when Mark called me back two days later, he told me better news than I had predicted. He looked all over downtown *Ottawa* for Aaron and eventually found him roaming the streets hanging out with some homeless people.

"He was all messed up on drugs and refused to come with me at first," Mark said. "I finally convinced him to go to the *Mood Disorder Centre of Ottawa*. I figured that was the best place for him.

"That's good to hear Mark," I said.

"Once we got there, they told us that they worked with patients and their families to understand the importance of treating the disorder and how vital it is that continuing care is essential for preventing recurrences of abnormal moods," said Mark. "Aaron actually listened to what they had to say. After being on the streets, I think he realizes that he needs help. He had to be the one to recognize that he is addicted to drugs and that he needs to get off them before he can improve his own life. He made an appointment to go back to discuss treatment options."

"Oh, Mark," I said. "That's really great news. We are all rooting for Aaron. With the right diagnosis and medication, you'll see that he'll be a new person in no time at all."

I thought to myself that Aaron would be fine as long as he stuck to the treatment plan that would be administered for him. That feeling in the pit of my stomach returned as I thought, *what would the future hold for Aaron if he did not?*

CHAPTER TWENTY-SIX

Huntsville

An e-mail arrived from Lynn about three months after she moved up to *Huntsville* after her retirement. She cheered the day that her husband Doug had finally made more than ten bucks an hour after two years of working hard in his business. She danced a jig when within five years in total he had made enough money so that they could retire and move up north to a more peaceful place.

Dear Jeanette:

I miss you and wish you were here. So much has happened in a short time since we left London. I don't know where to start. I'd like to tell you all the good news first but there's some bad news too. I guess I should start from the top down.

Son #1, Brian and Jessie are getting married. That is my exciting news. It only took eight years for them to realize it was the right thing for them. Jessie's sickness did put a damper on their marriage plans for the last couple of years but her cancer has gone into remission so they finally decided to get married. We are so happy for both of them.

Son #2, Barry and Amanda have split up and gone their separate ways after five years of marriage. Too much of the fast-paced life caught up to them. I'm really sad about the break-up because I love Amanda. It's hard when you love your daughter-in-law and a break up occurs. I thought they were right for each other but the lifestyle in California didn't do them any justice. I wished so much that Barry had listened to me all those years ago to stay in Canada and live a simpler life here but as you know, you can only advise your children so much and then you have to shut-up and leave the rest up to them. Barry is crushed that Amanda has found a new guy and I really hate to see him this way. He gave up everything for her when he moved 3540 kilometres away from home to marry her after only knowing her a few months. It was love at first sight and he gave up his family, friends, a good job and his citizenship to be with her, only now to be left with nothing but empty dreams

Son#3, Billy still has a harem of women following him wherever he goes but no real love interest. He is still living at home so we are not quite 'empty-nesters' yet. It feels good to still have a bit of commotion in the house by having him around but I'm worried he'll never get out. He's thirty-one now and looking too comfortable in his surroundings.

Doug is doing great but misses London. For what reason, I'll never know. He's not good with change as you know. I think he'll settle into the life up here in Huntsville once he realizes that it's the best life. I love it! He hates the winter up here and has real trouble with his allergies in this 'swampland' as he calls it. I am waiting for his happiness to catch up to him!

Now, what about me you say? I'm sad about Barry and Amanda. I'm happy about Brian and Jessie. I'm worried about Billy. I have no concerns about Doug. I'm excited about a new life up here in paradise. I'm missing you and your Doug. I can't wait to hear your news.

Never give up your dreams,
Love Lynn

I replied to Lynn as soon as I got her e-mail and wrote:

Dear Lynn:

So much has happened here too. Let me run through the list with you.

Son#1, Nicholas and Laura are doing fine. They seem very compatible and I hope that they will get married one day soon. Nick bought a four-plex apartment and is fixing it up to rent it out. He is keeping busy with all his businesses on the go.

Son#2, Peter and Sky are doing alright. At times their relationship seems a bit shaky since Peter is on the road a lot with his band. Being apart is not always good for the soul. He's trying to convince her to come with him on tour so they won't be apart so much. So far so good with them though.

Daughter #1, Jennie is getting married this summer at Rock Lake in Algonquin Park. As you know, Jordan wasn't our first choice for Jennie but you have to bite your tongue and just go along with the flow. She has planned the whole day and is only having close family and a few friends attend. We'll come by for a visit, of course, to see you and Doug in Huntsville while we are up there. I am still SO jealous of you moving up there while I am still stuck down here. Doug and I agreed to wait until Jennie was out of the house before we move up to Huntsville. I don't want her to go but it means our freedom at last to live closer to Algonquin (and to you too, of course!)

How am I doing? I'm so sad to hear about Barry and Amanda. I'm happy about Brian and Jessie. I'm apprehensive about Jennie and Jordan. I'm a little worried about Peter and Sky. I have no concerns about Doug (other than his usual health issue). I'm excited about moving up north sometime soon, I hope! I miss you and your Doug also. I can't wait to see you this summer!

Friends to the end,
Love Jeanette

CHAPTER TWENTY-SEVEN

Jennie's Wedding

I was happy for Maria when she and Leon had finally bought a house together out in the country. They had struggled for so many years while dealing with Seth and all of his troubles with the law that they had not had a normal family life and they had almost broken up several times because of it. Seth had driven a wedge between them and now that he was arrested and put in jail, there was a time of relief but this new sensation would not last long.

Maria told me that although she was not happy about the situation that Seth had found himself to be in, she was at least free from the constant worry of not knowing where he was and what he was doing. There was some solace in knowing now where he was, even if that meant jail.

I thought that it must have been difficult for Maria though in her efforts to correct his unruly behaviour all through the years when Seth was growing up. The constant suspensions from school, the visits to so many different doctors and psychiatrists and finally the visits to jail had taken its toll on her mental health. Maria had taken a leave of absence from work and was prescribed anti-depressants by her psychiatrist to help her cope with her moods.

Once Maria's own medication for depression took effect and they moved from their townhouse into an actual house that had a yard and garden, she seemed to be happier than she had been in a very long time.

"Finally, I can get away from these nosey neighbours," she told me. "I'm sure they are happy that we are leaving as well. Most nights were filled with yelling and screaming when Seth used to have his tantrums and punch holes in the walls of his bedroom. Both Leon and I tried to keep him under control but he was next to impossible to handle."

"That doesn't sound like it was ever very much fun Maria," I said to her.

"No it wasn't. I am really afraid now to be in the same room with Seth when his violent outbursts occur," she said. "Both Leon and Emily are also looking forward to a new start in life. I just hope we can keep it together. It's been quite the strain on all of us these last couple of years."

"Yes, us too with Doug's sickness and since surgery, it's been a struggle for all of us too," I said. "Now it's time to live it up."

"We bought a small trailer and two kayaks and were thinking of going camping at *Algonquin Park* this fall when Jennie gets married there," said Maria.

"That sounds great," I replied. "You know we'll be there at *Rock Lake* as usual. Peter is taking a break from touring and is working until late fall on contract as a warden up in *Algonquin* this year so it'll be great to see him in his element."

"I haven't been up to *Algonquin Park* since the time that you came by yourself all those years ago. I think Richard didn`t go with you since he went instead to go see his friend in *Quebec*. No one seemed to miss him much on that trip," she said. "Do you remember that little hike we did on the *Highland Trail*?"

"Don't you mean the *Highland Backpacking Trail*?" I questioned. "Yes, I remember that it wasn`t so little. It was nineteen kilometres long as I recall and it was intended to be done by serious overnight backpackers, not daytime hikers like us. I also remember all the up and down parts of the trail wreaked havoc on my neck. I also wasn't used to hiking for that many kilometres and it aggravated the whiplash I have in my neck. I remember being in a lot of pain but it was still worth it since we were in the beauty of *Algonquin*."

"How is your whiplash now Jeanette?" Maria asked. "Does it still bother you very much?"

"Yes, it does. I have arthritis in my neck now and the muscle spasms give me headaches. I really wish I could get a neck transplant but there is no such thing, of course." I said. "I just have to put up with the pain. At least I got rid of my other pain, years ago," I said in reference to Richard.

"You said it. Richard never supported you financially or emotionally for that matter," said Maria. "How many times has he been married now?"

"He's on his third marriage now," I said. "I'm not sure how he could have managed to rope in that many women to marry him but he obviously has some charm so it seems."

"He has the charm of a dead fish," said Maria. "No offence but I never particularly liked Richard very much and I thought you were way too good for him Jeanette."

"Well, the only good thing I got out of that marriage was Nick," I said.

"Well, at least Doug likes camping but I'm not so sure about you," she said as she laughed making reference to the fact that Doug had doubted that I liked camping when we first met.

"Doug finally knows that I'm a true camper after all these years, although, now that we are getting a little older, I don't think I would go back to camping in a tent anymore," I confessed. "I love the comfort of our fifth-wheel trailer and all the luxuries that it has. I'm glad you bought a trailer too and will be coming to *Algonquin* with us."

"Yes, I am too," said Maria. "I'm looking forward to going to Jennie's wedding as well."

"Yes," I said. "Doug is still a little upset that Jennie isn't getting married in a church but at least she'll be married by a minister."

"I can't think of a better place for a wedding than in *Algonquin*, other than *Hawaii*, of course," said Maria.

"If I ever get married again, so help me God, I want it to be in *Hawaii* and only if it was to *Steve McGarrett* from the new show *Hawaii Five-O*," I joked with Maria.

"He's a hunk, for sure," said Maria. "Now that I know your fantasy, do you want to know mine?"

"I'm almost afraid to ask," I said to Maria.

"Picture me with *Arnold Schwarzenegger* on *Bora-Bora Island* in the *French Polynesian Island* which is well known as *Paradise on Earth*," said Maria.

"That's a nice spot but with Arnold? He's not even your type," I chuckled. "If only Doug and Leon could hear us now. What would they say?"

"I'm sure they have their own fantasies too," said Maria. "As long as they keep it as such, we have nothing to worry about. We should plan for all of us to go on a trip together someday soon to the *Caribbean*."

"That sounds like a great idea but keep dreaming Maria," I said to her. "In the meantime, let's keep our fantasies on the back burner and stick to real life and enjoy *Algonquin Park* since it's the only real paradise that I know."

Jennie's wedding day turned out to be a perfect day as we gathered for the ceremony at *Rock Lake*. The hills were filled with colourful fall leaves, the water was crystal clear and the air was fresh. Jennie looked so beautiful and her fiancé Jordan looked at her with awe.

I turned to Doug and said, "He's looking at her the way you looked at me on our wedding day."

"I hope they can keep their promise to love each other for ever as we have. These days, it's harder than ever to stick together. The young kids today treat marriage like it's made with *Velcro*. If things don't go their way, they just pull it apart so easily," said Doug.

"I have my reservations about the two of them getting married as well but as you know, we can't say too much," I said as I gave Doug a concerned look. "I hate it when I get these feelings but as you know Jennie insists that Jordan is the one for her. She's dated many guys over the years and although she has unintentionally broken a lot of hearts along the way, I just hope that her heart doesn't get broken. She says she loves Jordan so there's not much we can do to change that."

"There's something I don't trust about him. We are here now and it's her choice so we have to stick with that decision of hers whether we like it or not," said Doug. "I'd like to re-new our wedding vows while we're here Jeanette. I can ask the minister to stay an extra day and we'll call Lynn and Doug to see if they'll come and be our witnesses. What do you say?"

"Do you mean that? You're so romantic Doug but I don't have anything to wear," I said as I gave Doug a big hug.

"We can go into *Huntsville* tomorrow and buy something and be ready to re-new those vows then," said Doug.

"Well, I can't think of a better place to renew them than up here in paradise!" I said.

"I'll take that as a YES then!" exclaimed Doug.

Chapter Twenty-Eight
Saying Good-bye

For the next few years, camping at *Algonquin Park* became more special than ever. I had fond memories of coming here when the kids were little and Peter was lucky to be on contract as Warden of the Park for the summers. This allowed him to be with nature in between the time that he toured with his band. Jennie ended up coming to camp alone while Jordan was visiting friends. He didn't like to camp but Jennie decided to come up and spend some time in the one place that truly brought her some happiness. Doug and I were also happy to keep returning to the special place where we had renewed our wedding vows.

When Jennie showed up, I asked her about the bruise on her face. "What happened honey?"

"I bumped into the bathroom cabinet. I'm such a klutz you know just like you Mom," she said.

"Well, I won't argue with you there but you need to be more careful dear," I said to her.

There were several other families who returned year after year to *Algonquin* once they discovered the camp and would arrive at the same time of the year to enjoy the peace and tranquility here. We really got to know our fellow campers and became good friends with several of the families.

Each family came from different parts of *Southwestern Ontario* and each gathered at camp with joys and sorrows of their own. Everyone seemed to enjoy the great outdoors for the same reasons that we did. I felt fortunate to come to *Algonquin* year after year and to forget about the outside world and all the troubles for a while.

There was one older *Dutch* fellow, named Hendrik Van Brock, who had been coming to *Rock Lake* for the past fifty-three years. He was now ninety-one years of age and even came alone after his wife died from cancer over fifteen years ago. He told us that he had seven grown children and never felt old until one day his youngest son advised him that he was applying for his old age pension.

"Now that I tell you, makes you feel old," said Hendrik.

He went on to tell us that it was difficult at first to come alone to camp without his wife but the sheer beauty of nature in the Park here was a strong attraction that he could not resist.

"I have had so many fond memories of camping here with my family in the past," said Hendrik. "Now it is time to build up new memories for many years to come, I hope!"

"You're an inspiration to all of us Hendrik," I said to him. "I'm impressed that you still come here all alone at your age. With all of us here though, you're not really alone."

"That's correct. I wouldn't miss this for anything in the world," he said. "Did you hear about the guy who was granted a wish from *God* for being a good man all his life?" he asked. "*The man said to God, I have always wanted to go to Hawaii but I am deathly afraid to fly, so I wish you could build me a bridge there. God said, No I can't fulfill that wish, it's too difficult, but you may have another wish. Then the man said, Okay, please God, I have been married and divorced three times in my life and I wish you could help me to understand women. And then God said, Would you like one lane or two?*"

We all laughed out loud at this joke; even though he had told the same joke last year and didn't seem to realize it. It was a joke that was funny even the second time that I heard it. At his age of ninety-one, I was not only impressed that he simply remembered the joke but that he told it so well.

While we were all gathered around the big circle campfire that night with our fellow campers, there was a ruckus that occurred out at the water. We were all having a good time roasting marsh mellows, eating *smores* and telling stories. It was a starlit night and the moon was out in full glory. There was a path of light reflecting on the water from the moon that illuminated the camp without the need to use flashlights.

I suddenly heard a rustling along the beach and looked up to see what it might be. Ordinarily, you wouldn't be able to see that far without the glow of the moon. Doug stood up first and said, "Don't anyone move. Stay where you are." As he said this, a shot was fired and screams were heard.

"What was that?" cried Jennie.

"Not to worry," said Doug. "I'll go and investigate."

A crowd had gathered out at the water's edge and there was a black lump lying in the sand. Peter stood over a black bear and told everyone to stay back.

"Everything's under control," Peter said in a very commanding voice. "The bear is not harmed. It is tranquilized and will be transported to the interior away from the campsites here. Unfortunately, this is the second sighting and capture of this bear this summer. If we catch this bear poking around for a third time, we will have to destroy it."

"You can't do that," said one person in the crowd.

"We have no choice," Peter went on to explain. "Typically, black bears do not pose a threat if they fear humans but once that fear has been removed, they become a danger. These are beautiful animals and believe me; I would do anything not to have to put any one of them down."

"Why can't you just take them far away?" asked another person in the crowd.

"There's so little territory left for the black bear around here. We have taken so much of their natural habitat away from them. A single male black bear requires a minimum thirty-five square kilometre range to live in to survive. It's sad that these magnificent animals have nowhere to go," said Peter. "Someone has left fish guts here in the bushes I see that has attracted the bear to the camp. It is imperative to dispose of all attractants in the proper containers to keep this from happening again."

"I can't believe people can be so dumb," said Doug. "Leaving fish guts around is the same as leaving candy out for a baby."

"Well sir, you're right," said Peter as he gave his Dad a wink. "A bear has an excellent sense of smell which is twenty-one hundred times better than humans. Even a dog's sense of smell is only one-hundred times better than humans. Bears can be attracted to smells from as far away as thirty-two kilometres."

Doug looked very proud as he walked back to our campsite. "Peter is doing well working with the wild animals in the Park," said Doug. "He is dedicated to educating people to co-exist with these wonderful animals. Peter certainly has a love for animals and nature in general."

"We taught him well," I said to Doug when he sat back down around the campfire.

"Yes, we did," said Doug. "Too bad others haven't taught their children the same. Can you believe those young guys that left yesterday? They skinned their fish and left the guts down by the water in the bushes. It's pure ignorance."

"They seemed like nice guys but they were from *Toronto*. You know those city slickers come up here and have no clue how to respect nature," I said. "We should bundle up the fish guts and send it in the mail to them and see if that would teach them anything."

"That's a waste of time Jeanette," Doug said. "Better yet, it would be great to send the bear after them and watch them scramble."

When it was our turn to leave paradise behind for yet another year and return home, it was difficult to say good-bye to our friends and to know that we would all have to wait another whole year to see one another again. It was back to reality and dealing with everyday issues again.

Once we were home, I got a phone call from Jennie saying that she had hurt herself and that she was at the hospital and needed me to pick her up.

"Are you alright?" I asked. "Where is Jordan?"

"He's working at the construction site in *Kitchener* and can't pick me up. Can you just come and get me Mom, please?" she pleaded.

"Of course, Jennie, I'll be right there," I said.

When I arrived at the hospital, I was dismayed to see that Jennie's arm was in a cast.

"What happened to you Jennie?" I asked.

"I fell down the stairs this morning," she said. "I had my hands full and tripped on the cat and tumbled down and hit my head too but I'm alright. Please just take me home Mom."

"Are you sure, you're alright Jennie?" I asked.

"I'm fine, Mom. Just a little dizzy," she said.

As I took Jennie to her townhouse, my mind started to question her story about falling down the stairs.

"Jennie, if Jordan is hurting you . . . ," I said to her and then I thought to myself, *I'll kill him.*

"No Mom, really I fell and landed on my arm," she insisted. "I know to be more careful in the future."

After making sure Jennie was settled at her townhouse, I went home and told Doug what my fears were about the situation with Jennie.

"When I asked her if Jordan was hurting her, she denied it but she didn't seem insulted by my suggestion that he was hurting her. She just said that she would have to be more careful in the future. I don't know what to think Doug. I really hope he's not hurting her," I said.

"Well, he had better hope that he's not hurting her or I'll hurt him," Doug said angrily.

"Don't worry Doug. If that's the case, Mama Bear will get to him first," I said sternly.

The next day Doug had a doctor's appointment at the cancer clinic. When we arrived we were immediately told that Doug had become immune to the medication that he was on and his cancer had returned. Doctor Maynard said that he was hesitant to operate this time since the cancer had spread and his odds of surviving the operation let alone stopping the further spread of the disease was minimal.

Doug and I shared a look that was filled with an understanding but it was difficult to think about saying good-bye. His luck had run out. He was sixty years old now and thin as a rake without much energy left. He fought the good fight and got twelve extra years from the time that he was first diagnosed with this disease. I was truly thankful for those extra years that we had together.

"I don't want to say good-bye Jeanette so I'll just say see you later," said Doug. "We'll meet again someday and I want you to promise me that you'll get married again. You're still young and sexy baby."

"Do you think I want to torture myself by getting married ever again? No way, you're my soul mate so there's no-one else that could even come close to fulfilling my needs," I replied back to Doug.

"I want you to be happy Jeanette, you deserve it," said Doug.

"I'll be fine on my own, don't you worry about me Doug," I said. "Let's have a glass of wine in bed and have a toast to our life together. Remember we did the same thing the night before your surgery."

"I remember doing something else as well that night baby," replied Doug. "Drink up and let's get to it."

Three months later, Doug became very weak and I tried to convince him that he should go to the hospital to get the proper care that he needed but he refused to go.

"Let me go in peace at home. I only want you to take care of me like you always have Jeanette," he said as I was holding his hand in bed. "I hope you don't mind?"

"No, of course I don't mind," I said. "I'll do anything for you. Let me know what you need."

Doug laughed and gave me a look and asked, "You know what I need baby?"

"Alright, besides that, of course," I said as I smiled at him.

It wasn't long after that when I gave Doug a hug and a kiss that I felt him slip away. It was an uneasy feeling to listen as he took his last breath. I had not only lost a husband, friend and partner but a piece of my paradise died with him. My heart was beating to a broken tune now. I suddenly felt a shudder go through my body and felt so utterly all alone.

I poured myself a glass of wine and as I drank it, I felt numb all over. I cried and felt the world stand still for a while. I had never truly been alone in my life. I thought about how my life started out with my twin sister in my mother's womb and how I lived with my family at home until I was married. My father moved in with me after my divorce, and Doug and I were then married for twenty-five years. It suddenly felt terrifying to feel all alone and have no-one now to take care of. I missed Doug so much but I knew I had to lay him to rest in the best place that I knew.

Chapter Twenty-Nine

Spreading the Ashes

Nick grew to become a handsome young man full of confidence and maturity. He was an entrepreneur and dabbled in the real estate market along with his website design business. Peter and Sky moved in next door to Nick into one of four apartments that he owned in a four-plex building. I was proud of Nick for going to college and doing so well for himself considering what he had gone through with his mental state in his early teenage years. To look at him now, he seemed perfectly normal yet there was a vulnerable side to him. Although he was stable while he stayed on his medication, there was always the fear in the back of my mind that he wouldn't always be this way.

When he first met Laura MacLean, he was very cautious about revealing his bi-polar disorder to her since he didn't want to scare her away by letting her know about this skeleton from his closet. He came to me one day after he met Laura and had dated her for a few months and asked, "Mom, what should I do? I want to let Laura know about my condition but I don't want her to run for the hills afterwards. We have all heard horror stories about people who are bi-polar going off their meds and becoming these depressed monsters. I love her a lot and just want to be with her."

"Well Nick, you have to gather up the strength to tell her the truth if you are that serious about her," I said to him. "Just make sure you speak to her from the heart and let her decide if she wants to spend the rest of her life with you or not after knowing this about you."

"I know I have to tell her Mom but I'm dreading it," he said.

Nick invited me over the next day for tea and told me that he finally was able to tell Laura about his condition. He was surprised to hear her say that she understood all about the illness since her uncle, Luke MacLean, was also bi-polar. Nick told me that before he was diagnosed, he used to be considered lazy by everyone in the family and he dropped out of high school and left the house at age sixteen. He ended up living under a bridge in *New York City* and gathered up pop bottles to help pay for his drug and booze habits. No-one ever thought much about him and wrote him off from the family.

"Literally, he had hallucinations and thought that he was seeing an angel one day," said Nick. "This angel turned out to be a social worker from *St. Paul's Catholic Church* who approached him on the street while he was looking for pop bottles. When she asked him about his accent, he told her that he was originally from *Niagara Falls, Canada* but somehow ended up in *New York* and couldn't remember how he got there. She ended up taking him back to the church and offered him a hot meal along with giving his dignity back."

"So what happened next?" I asked Nick.

"He was admitted to a mental hospital and was treated for his condition. Her uncle Luke was lucky that someone took an interest in helping him for the first time in his life instead of turning him away and calling him worthless," said Nick. "She also told me that her uncle went back to school to become of all things, a psychologist and now he helps others cope with their disorders."

"That's amazing that he has done so well considering he once lived under a bridge," I said to Nick.

"Yes, he was misdiagnosed as a misfit in his younger days and treated with total disrespect. He was considered lazy and stupid and none of that was true," said Nick.

"So, Laura didn't think any less of you?" I asked Nick.

"No, she did not at all Mom. She understood that my condition once treated is manageable," Nick said. "She just asked me to promise her that I would stay on my medication. I told her that I already knew how important that is and I told her all about my experience with becoming catatonic."

"That's wonderful Nick," I said. "Where is Laura tonight?"

"She had to leave after dinner to go to work at *St Joseph's Hospital*," said Nick. "She was just transferred to the neonatal unit where she gets to hold babies all night. She was looking forward to that."

"That's great Nick," I said. "Laura sounds like she is a very understanding and caring person. You too are a sweet man who knows how to treat a woman. I know you two will be happy together."

"I have a surprise for her when I take her out for dinner tomorrow night," said Nick.

The peace and quiet was suddenly interrupted by an argument that was coming from next door and then a door slammed and someone stomped out of the apartment. Then I heard a knock on Nick's door and suddenly, there stood Peter in the doorway looking very casual but frustrated.

"Hey bro what's up? How are you doing Mom?" asked Peter. "I didn't know you were here."

"I'm fine," I said to Peter.

"Things are good with me also bro," said Nick. "I am going to ask Laura to marry me tomorrow night. What about you and Sky? What's going on in paradise next door?"

"Hardly paradise dude," said Peter. "I love her and want to marry her but she keeps fucking forgetting, sorry about the swearing Mom, to take her meds and it's slowly killing me. I want her to come on tour with me but she's refusing saying it's too lonely for her while I'm busy with the band."

"Yeah, she's probably right you know," said Nick. "Why don't you just cut her some slack and see what happens or cut her off for good this time."

"It's not that easy when you love someone and I'm back on the road again tomorrow for another tour, so we'll see how things go once I'm back," said Peter. "Have you heard anything from Jennie lately?"

"She is going with Mom tomorrow to *Algonquin* to spread Dad's ashes," said Nick.

"Oh, I forgot about that," said Peter. "I hope that goes well for you Mom." Peter came over to me and gave me a big hug.

"Thanks Pete," I said to him. "I hope everything goes well on tour. Do you think Sky will be back?"

"Well, I don't know. She has to find her own paradise in life. I thought that included me but I don't know anymore," said Peter. "Well, take it easy Mom and congratulations Nick on your engagement to Laura. That's if she accepts, of course! She's awesome! See you in another couple of months."

While Peter was back on the road again, Jennie and I were on the road to *Algonquin* the next day to spread Doug's ashes in *Rock Lake*.

He and I had both talked about wanting to be laid to rest there in the middle of paradise. At first I wanted to go alone but Jennie insisted that she come with me to help spread the ashes. She was always such a great support for me since Doug passed away.

"I want you to promise me that when I pass on, that you'll spread my ashes here along with Dad so that our paradise will be complete," I said to Jennie. "I hope that's not too much to ask?"

"I can do that Mom," she said. "I know you two old lovebirds want to be together out here, forever."

"Thanks Jennie," I said. "Now speaking of lovebirds, how are things going between you and Jordan?"

"Not so good Mom. He gets so jealous whenever any guy even just looks at me. He gets very angry with me and it scares me. I love him but I'm not happy with how he treats me sometimes," she said sadly. "He can be so charming at times but then if the house isn't perfectly clean when he gets home he gets enraged. What should I do Mom?"

"Well, Jennie, if he's hurting you in more ways than one, you don't have to take that. You need to make a choice now. If he has crossed the line, you need to leave him," I went on to explain.

"He has hurt me Mom but he always says he's sorry and brings me flowers. I'm sure he won't hurt me again," said Jennie.

"Oh Jennie, you only have one life to live and it's too short to put up with that nonsense," I said to her.

"He can be very sweet to me though Mom. He makes me dinner and buys me things," she said softly. "He says that he loves me so everything should be alright."

While we stood in front of *Rock Lake* and as I gave her a big hug, the sun fell into the water and we heard the call of a loon that echoed out over the lake.

As I spread the ashes over the water, the sky was lit up with beautiful glowing bands of red and orange colours. I smiled and said, "It's time to say good-bye Doug. I love you."

Then Jennie said as she waved, "Good-bye Daddy. I miss you."

Then the thought occurred to me, *good-bye Jordan. I will come up with a plan so that we can all say good-bye to you and no-one will miss you!*

CHAPTER THIRTY

Obsession

Aaron got caught up in a life of selfishness. He stopped caring about his family and friends. He became obsessed with his image of becoming a body builder. He left *Ottawa* and headed out to *Las Vegas* to seek a life of fortune and fame. He was mesmerized by the thought of body building and the glitter of the fast life in *Vegas*. This led him to a life of drugs and running around with prostitutes. It wasn't the type of life that you would want for your child and even though he was twenty five years old now and knew better, he acted so recklessly.

When Mark told me that Aaron stopped taking his medication and that his addictive personality had won out over any reasoning with him, I wasn't surprised at all. Aaron did not understand the ramifications of going off his medication and altering his mind with illegal drugs or he simply did not care.

"I know I've said this before, he needs to stay on his medication before something drastic happens," I said compassionately.

"The problem is that his addictive personality makes it hard for him to control his behaviour whether it's about gambling, drugs or sex," Mark went on to say. "It's been a battle and I'm not sure I can help him with this problem anymore."

"Don't give up on him Mark," I said. "He needs you now more than ever."

"I know that Jeanette. I really don't want to give up on him at all but it's just very difficult to convince him that he is headed for a downward spiral that isn't going to be very easy to reverse," said Mark. "He blames all of his problems on his unhappy childhood."

"What is he thinking?" I questioned. "You have done everything for him."

"I know," said Mark. "We not only put a roof over his head and fed him but we signed him up for everything from swimming lessons, skiing and soccer and we always took him on fun family vacations. He says that he wasn't happy because we moved around too much when he was growing up and he told me that his Mom used to beat on him when I was away at sea."

"I never knew that Mark," I said. "Why did she do that?"

"I don't know," said Mark. "I guess she had an alcoholic father who used to beat her and he kicked her out of the house when she was only sixteen years old, so she has her own issues. I told her, I didn't like it that she hit him but she always said he was hard to handle and since I was away at sea, it was difficult for her to deal with him on her own."

"Still, that's not right, Mark," I said. "Doug had an alcoholic father too but he chose to stop the violence and never hit the kids."

"Yes," said Mark. "There's never a good excuse to hit your kids. I didn't find out until later, when Aaron was older. I guess that's one of the reasons why he hates his mother."

"It doesn't help the situation, that's for sure," I said sympathetically. "It only exasperates an already bad situation."

"I agree," said Mark. "I think it's all too late now."

The tragic news came three days later. Aaron had been drinking heavily one night while in a *Las Vegas* hotel and had overdosed on drugs. The combination was lethal. It was sad to lose yet another life in the family to reckless behaviour that was brought on by mental illness. It was a defeat that was hard to accept, especially for my brother Mark who tried so hard to help Aaron fight this wicked illness.

I decided to go visit Maria to see how she was managing now after Seth had been sentenced and to tell her the sad news about Aaron. When I got to her place it was a disaster. It didn't look like she had done any dishes or laundry for weeks. I didn't say anything to her about my observations when she answered the door in her t-shirt and sleep pants. Her hair was a big mess also and it was sticking up all over the place. She told me that she wasn't feeling great but that I could come in for tea if I wanted. She said to excuse the mess and started to tell me that Emily had left for *Australia*.

"What is she doing there?" I asked.

"She met a guy named Samuel Campbell and left with him to visit *Australia*. He is a herpetologist studying reptiles in the great *Tanami Desert*. Emily is enjoying the scenery, rocks, gorges and coloured sands there. She's been to the coast as well and has gone swimming with the dolphins. You know those are her favourite animals and she has always wanted to do that. I think it will be good for her to be away. Maybe it will make her a little more independent."

"I hope so Maria. I think Peter will be a little jealous to hear that she is visiting the place where his bearded dragon comes from," I said.

"I'm sure he'll get to tour there one day when he becomes even more famous than he is now. It's so sad to hear about Aaron though," said Maria. "He was a good kid but he didn't know how to help himself. It's really awful that he didn't stay on the medication that he so desperately needed to have normalcy."

"He didn't want normal," I said. "Mark told me that Aaron didn't like feeling so flat while he was on his medication. He missed the highs of his mania and went off the medication and substituted illegal drugs and alcohol to try to get to that level again. Nothing even came close to the highs that he felt from being bi-polar."

"Wow, I never thought about it that way before," said Maria. "That explains why I always felt better when I smoked pot but once it wore off, I would come crashing down."

"Well, you're lucky you never used hard drugs Maria. Aaron came crashing down really hard this time and there's no bouncing back from that," I said. "He was obsessed with himself and became his own worst enemy."

"I know the feeling Jeanette," said Maria. "It's not pleasant to loose your child to senseless acts. I feel like I've already lost one who is behind bars and I'm not sure what's in store for the other one."

"To be honest with you Maria, I came over because the ring that Mom gave me is missing ever since Emily was over to our house the last time," I said. "I don't care that she took it. It means a lot to me so I just want it back."

"Well, she didn't take it Jeanette," said Maria as she looked down to the ground. "I did."

"What the hell?" I shouted at her. "I want it back now."

"I don't have it right now," said Maria. "I pawned it Jeanette. I needed the money."

"What for this time Maria?" I asked. "Dope as usual?"

"No. This time it is for a legitimate reason," said Maria.

"That ring has sentimental value since it's a family heirloom that Mom gave to me on my eighteenth Birthday!" I said. "I want to give it to Jennie. What did you do with your ring?"

"I sold it years ago when I was in *Vancouver*," she said. "I needed the money to survive at the time."

"Well, I'm really pissed off Maria," I said. "When can I get it back?

"I hope I will get it back to you next week. I'm really sorry," she said.

"Well, I hope so," I said to her. "Why didn't you just get the money you needed from Leon?" I asked.

"He left a couple of weeks ago and isn't coming back," said Maria. "You would think that after all these fucking years of dealing with Seth's problems, now that he is in prison, that Leon could be happy now. Well, he told me that the wedge that Seth put in our relationship was too large to mend. He doesn't love me anymore and so now that Emily has left also, I am truly all alone."

"I'm really sorry to hear that Maria," I said to her. Now tell me why you needed the money."

"It's a long story but I needed the money to fly my daughter home from *Vancouver*," said Maria.

"What are you talking about?" I asked. "I thought you said Emily was in *Australia*?"

"She is," said Maria. "I'm talking about Larissa. I never told you that while I was in *Vancouver*, I got pregnant and gave my baby up for adoption. It bothered me all these years not to have had any contact with her so I finally did make contact and she's coming here to see me next week."

"Was Larry the father?" I asked.

"No, Rocco Ricardo was," she said. "He was a chapter member of the *Hell's Angels Bike Club* in *Vancouver*. I met him in a bar after Larry dumped me. Once Rocco knew I was pregnant, he wanted me to have an abortion but I left him and had my baby all on my own and then gave her up. It wasn't an easy choice to make but for the baby's sake, it was the right thing to do. I never said anything to anyone in the family and the guilt has eaten away at me all these years."

"Well Maria," I said. "I am glad that you are able to meet Larissa after all of these years. I just hope it all goes well. Do you need some help to clean up the awful mess?"

"No, I can do it myself Jeanette," she said. "I promise you, I'll get that ring back also."

"Don't worry about it Maria," I said to her. "Just make sure that you clean the place up before Larissa comes for a visit. First impressions can mean a lot."

"How is Jennie doing?" asked Maria. "Didn't the two of you just come back from *Algonquin*?"

"Yes, we just got back late last night and Jennie is still sleeping at my place," I said. "She didn't want to wake Jordan up since he had to get up early and go to work in *Kitchener* on the construction site. I'm really worried about her though. I think Jordan has been beating on her," I confessed. "I should go soon and give her a ride back home."

"Jennie's a smart, beautiful and strong girl," said Maria. "I think she can take care of herself. You worry too much you know."

"Well, I think Jordan will have to be the one to worry now," I said to Maria. I told Maria all about my plan.

CHAPTER THIRTY-ONE

Ice

When I dropped Jennie off at her townhouse, Jordan was already home waiting for her. He had made a wonderful candle light dinner for the two of them but he looked a little annoyed as Jennie got out of the car.

"Will you be alright Jennie?" I asked her in a low voice.

"I'll be fine Mom," said Jennie. "Don't worry so much."

"Hi, Mrs. Bennett," said Jordan as he waved to me and turned to Jennie and asked, "How did the ashes thing go?"

"That is my father's ashes you're talking about Jordan. It was really hard to say good-bye. Mom here feels better though that he's at peace in their favourite place," she said. "See you later Mom. Have a good night."

"You too, Jennie," I said. "Thanks again for going with me."

As I left, I could hear Jordan say to Jennie, "It's your favourite, chicken fettuccine, all gluten-free with a salad and some _Chardonnay_ wine. I missed you sweetie while you were gone."

As I drove away, I thought to myself, _he is such a charmer. He had better hope that he's treating Jennie alright or else._

Once I got home and as I settled in for the night, I got a message from Jennie on my cell phone that read, *ICE*. My heart skipped a beat but I knew then that I had to put the plan into action. I called *911* and drove over to Jennie's townhouse as fast as I could. When I arrived, there were two police officers banging on her door and I heard one of them shout, "Open up the door, it's the police."

I started to tremble as I watched the police enter the townhouse and I could hear a scuffle that occurred. They quickly had Jordan into hand-cuffs and put him into the back of the cruiser. I ran past the police car and didn't even look at Jordan. As I went through Jennie's front door, I saw her sitting on the couch talking to a female officer.

"Excuse me but you can't come in here," said another officer.

"Jennie is my daughter," I said. "Please let me see her. Is she alright?"

"Mom," Jennie cried. "I'm alright. Just a little shaken up but I'm alright."

"You'll have to stay outside until we get a full statement from Jennie and then you can see her," said the officer.

After waiting for over ten gruelling minutes, I finally got to see Jennie and saw that she had a few bruises on her face and arm but overall she seemed to be doing alright.

"He won't hurt you any more Jennie," I said to her. "It's all over now." I thought to myself, *she is finally safe now and I will never let him ever come near her again.*

"Thanks Mom for calling the police," she said. "I'm glad you got my ICE message, In Case of Emergency. It was a great way to let you know that I was in trouble. I pressed charges against Jordan so he's going to jail."

Then as Jennie's eyes started to fill with tears, so did mine. She told me that Jordan had accused her of having an affair with a colleague at work. He got so angry with her that he slammed her into a wall and instead of fighting back like she always did which only enraged him more, Jennie ran to her room and sent me the text message.

"Don't feel bad Jennie. He's going where he belongs," I said to her. "You're a strong person. Don't forget, I will be here for you to help you get through all of this and so will your brothers."

"I know Mom," she said as she cried. "It just hurts so much to think that he could do this to me. I thought he loved me and he would change but I know in my heart that he never will. Things were just getting worse each time."

"He's a very weak person Jennie if he has to resort to hitting such a beautiful woman like you," I said to her. "It's not your fault."

"I tried so hard to please him in so many ways but nothing was ever good enough," she said. "He is a very controlling person and now they have control of him. Let's see how he likes to be on ICE."

"I hope he freezes in there, Jennie," I said. "He won't like his freedom taken away from him either. At least you are free now and that's the way it should be. There are endless opportunities for you now."

The following summer, Jennie met Jimmy De Luc at the *Big Heavy Metal* concert when Peter and his band *Paradise Fears* were playing in *Toronto*. It was a big break for the band to be able to be lined up with one of the best heavy metal bands around, *Motorhead*. Jennie liked touring with Peter's band and she got to spend some extra time with Sky as well. Sky had finally decided to tour with Peter since Jennie would be there to keep her company. It was great for

Jennie to get away from *London* for a while and to forget about the problems that she had with Jordan. She seemed happy about going to visit the big City of *Toronto* and seeing what the night life was all about and that's when she met Jimmy.

Jimmy was a very handsome young doctor practicing medicine at the *Toronto Hospital for Sick Children.* Jennie sounded really excited when she called me from the motel room after the concert.

"Mom, he's wonderful," Jennie said. "He is very caring and is an excellent doctor and above all try to guess what he likes to do in his spare time?"

"He likes to listen to heavy metal music right?" I replied.

"That too but it's better than that," said Jennie. "He likes to go camping. I'm very excited but I'm also scared at the same time Mom. It's hard for me to trust again after all I went through with Jordan."

"I know that feeling honey," I confided to her. "Go with what your heart tells you but give yourself time to get to know him really well before you give him your whole heart. It's moments like this that you have to learn not to make the same mistake twice. Keep a piece of paradise in your heart honey and only share it with him once you are ready."

CHAPTER THIRTY-TWO

Seventy-Seven

As I got older, each year seemed to go by faster and faster. Life moved along at a pace that felt like it was in fast forward mode. *Was I not just turning fifty just yesterday and not liking it one bit?* I asked myself. A lot has happened since then. The world has changed over the last twenty-seven years at such a rapid pace and now I find myself in the year 2039. The world population is up over nine and a half billion people, there are robots doing our work, replicators that make our food and other essentials that we need which have helped to eliminate world hunger. Most diseases and illness have been eradicated thanks to the rapid increase in nanotechnology and best of all; people don't have to work as hard now so everyone has more time to spend with their families.

Nicholas and Laura ended up having two wonderful children, Devon and Charlotte who are ten and eight years old now. They are living in the fun years stage of their lives when the kids are still young and not yet teenagers. Not that I have anything against teenagers, I used to be one of course many years ago but that was the age when mental illness seemed to be triggered in some of my unluckiest family members. I used to worry a great deal about the grand-children inheriting this illness from my side of the family. Internally, it made me happiest to know that mental illnesses have now been eradicated and there was no more worry about inheriting this wicked illness for future generations to come. In my eyes, this advancement alone was helping to make paradise on earth.

Peter and Sky managed to stick together but they didn't have any children. This allowed them to live a more carefree life and since they travelled on the road a lot, it would have been difficult anyway for them to have a normal family life. When Sky decided to keep traveling with Peter and his band, this kept their relationship vibrant while she was able to become one of his biggest fans.

I was elated that Jennie had found true happiness after she divorced Jordan and met Jimmy shortly after. Once they got married, they had two children, Betsy who is five years old and Dillon who is three years old. They are a very good-looking and happy family.

I never re-married in all those years after Doug passed away but ended up living next door to Maria. It was tragic when Maria got the news from *Australia* that Emily had lost her life in a car accident while living out there. Although Maria was vividly upset at her loss, she said that she felt lucky to have made contact with Larissa who had become a big part of her life. Larissa came for visits as often as she could to see Maria and she was always such a big support for her. Larissa was the one who helped me convince Maria to buy a place next door to me just like my Mom and *Tante* Wilma did all those years ago. That way we could keep an eye on one another but still have our privacy. She agreed and so we were back together again at the end just like when we first started out in life.

I almost found it hard to believe that Doug had been gone now for almost twenty years. After Doug's death, time stood still for me only for a short time and then the time seemed to take off along with all that technology. I still missed him as much today though as I did all those years ago.

Today, I found myself thinking way back to the day of the last camping trip that Doug and I spent together at *Rock Lake*. I'll never forget how wonderful that day was even though Doug was in a lot of pain. We had woken up early and had coffee and toast while sitting outside in front of our lake-front campsite. The day was beautiful without a cloud in the sky. The ducks were making their little quaking noises in the background and I said to Doug, "I feel like a millionaire sitting and enjoying the great view here in front of paradise."

"Well, I feel like a million bucks just spent," said Doug.

"Are you not feeling well today?" I asked Doug. I could tell he looked warn out and a bit grey in colour but I didn't want to say anything to him about that.

"I'm alright," he said.

I knew that was his standard answer when he really wasn't feeling well at all. "Let's go to the falls anyway. You never know when it'll be the last time we get to go and see them together," insisted Doug.

Doug started up the boat and away we travelled to the falls at *Pen Lake* which connected to *Rock Lake* at the far southern end. We passed a few canoeists and some fishermen trying to catch some lake trout. Once we reached the falls, I could hear the rushing waters and saw a moose in the distance feeding in the swamp to the far right. We hiked all around and saw other wild life including a beaver and a few great blue herons off in the marsh.

"I can't think of a greater day that I've had lately Doug," I commented to him. Doug just nodded his head but I could tell that he was in severe pain. He held his belly and said, "We should head back to base camp soon. I feel a bit light headed."

"No problem," I said to him. "While you rest, I can start dinner."

"I'm not hungry at all," moaned Doug.

I still have that picture in my mind of Doug giving me a half smile while enduring the pain that he had that day to make it a day worth remembering. I thought back also to the day that Doug and I renewed our vows at *Rock Lake*. These were all good memories of the last days that we shared at *Algonquin Park* and it was all that I had to hang onto.

My thoughts were suddenly brought back to the present when I arrived at Maria's place and was greeted with a boisterous roar of, "SURPRISE, HAPPY BIRTHDAY!" by a large group of people. Some faces I recognized and some I did not. Maria was grinning and gave me a look of excitement as all of these people had gathered around for the surprise party including Larissa.

"Is this twenty-nine or ninety-two?" I joked. I knew of course that it couldn't be twenty-nine but I also hoped that it wasn't ninety-two. *That's too old*, I thought.

"No, it's seventy-seven," said Peter. "One of your favourite numbers Mom. You can't get that one wrong!" Everyone laughed and it felt good to laugh. The room was filled with excitement and Peter and his band were there projected by hologram ready to play some music. It all seemed so real as if they were there in the room with us.

"This is such a wonderful surprise to see everyone, thank-you for coming," I said as the tears trickled down my face. I tried to wipe them away with the back of my hand but Jennie came to me with a *Kleenex*.

"Happy Birthday Mom and *Tante* Maria," said Jennie. "I have a special surprise for both of you today." Jennie handed me a gift and I opened it carefully. It was a picture of *Rock Lake* in *Algonquin Park* that she had painted, looking out at the trees, the lake and the hills. It was stunning and Maria gasped as she saw it. Jennie had entitled it, *Paradise at your Fingertips*. I cried again as I gave her a big hug.

"As you know Jennie, for your Dad and me, *Rock Lake* was our paradise. It was a special place where we could forget about all of our worries and be at peace. Before we even set up camp, we would walk up to the water, breath in the air and stretch out our hands and touch paradise with our fingertips. But now that I can't get there as often as I would like, it has a whole new meaning. Your fingertips brought paradise to me. Thank-you so much Jennie," I said as I cried tears of joy.

Jennie gave Maria a gift also. When she started unwrapping the present, I could see the tears starting to trickle down her cheeks. It was a portrait of Seth that she had painted entitled, *never forget*. He looked so dignified and handsome in the picture.

"You should keep him close to your heart *Tante* Maria. Don't forget about him," said Jennie. After Seth had died in the riot in prison, Maria had put away all of his pictures. She did not want to be reminded of all the pain that he had caused her over the years.

"I will do that Jennie, thank-you," she said.

Then it was Peter's turn to address the crowd. "Thanks for coming here today to celebrate my Mom's and *Tante* Maria's seventy-seventh birthday. We have a few songs to play for you in keeping with the rock and roll era that my Mom and *Tante* Maria grew up in. We are happy that we are able to be with you today and play some music all the way from *Amsterdam* where we have been touring. This one is for you *Tante* Maria, one of your all time favourites . . . *Whole Lotta Love,* by *Led Zeppelin.*"

Maria was elated and danced in her seat to the music. Everyone enjoyed the song and then Peter and his band slowed it down and played another song.

"Mom, this next song is dedicated to you and Dad. I wish he could be here today to celebrate with you. This one is called, *Another Day in Paradise*, by *Phil Collins.*

I tried to hide the tears while he sang this song but there was no stopping them. It reminded me of how lucky I was and all of my family to be able to live in paradise every day and not be out on the street with *nowhere to go and nothing to eat*. Part of my paradise was gone though after Doug had passed on but I managed to survive to seventy-seven so far and was here to celebrate the day in style.

One by one, we were greeted by other family and friends and each reminisced about the good times. It felt good to think about all of the good times that I had and not dwell on the negative.

My cousin John deValk reminded us about how much fun we had in the summer of 1981 when Maria and I went camping with him out west and back.

"We had lots of fun that summer but do you remember the day you almost gave us a heart attack John?" I asked.

"What time was that? Our trip was filled with so many moments hanging onto our hearts," said John.

"This was when you ran up ahead of us up on the trail at *Old Woman's Bay* and yelled out a cry in a frightened sounding voice. All we heard next was a big splash and when we looked down there were rings in the water. Both Maria and I looked horrified at each other, thinking that you had fallen off the cliff into the rocky bottom below but instead you were laughing your face off at the top of the cliff after throwing a big rock into the water. You watched us run all the way down the trail lightening fast to try and rescue you."

"That was a good one! How about the time we got lost and drove ten miles up that narrow logging road and met that hillbilly with his shotgun?" asked John. "He really gave me the creeps and I thought for sure that he was going to blow our heads off for trespassing. He was a real red-neck with scraggily long hair and several missing teeth and carried a shot gun that was pointed right at me."

"We quickly drove away and didn't look back. It definitely scarred me more than if we had come across seeing a grizzly bear in the mountains," said Maria. "The worst thing though that happened on our trip was when Jeanette almost got snatched by the *BC monster*. I'm glad he eventually got caught that summer in 1981 after we left and is rotting in prison for his crimes."

"There was only one other time on the trip that my whole nineteen years flashed before my eyes. I'll never forget standing along the edge of the gorge at *Hells Canyon* in *British Columbia*. It was hell alright when I lost my balance and almost flipped down the three-thousand foot drop to the bottom. Luckily, Mark was there to snatch me by my lucky spirit sand necklace and he saved me from going all the way over. Hey, where is Mark?" I asked.

I wanted to tell him thanks again for saving my life back then and thanks for being such a good brother but I forgot for a moment, I really hated when I did that, that he passed away last year from kidney failure. His one kidney burst when he was only twenty years old and stationed in *Esquimalt* on the west coast. He made it all those years with just one kidney but in the end it gave out and his body rejected any transplant.

When I realized what I was asking, I quickly went on to ask, "Remember the time that we saw Mark on the west coast during our trip? We got to tour the navy ship he was on and the *Naval Officers* poured us all those *navy-double* drinks and we ate salmon cooked on the open fire on the beach at the spit. Those were fun times except for when I threw up over the side of the ship, of course. The best part of all was when Mark had bought us all tickets to see an *Ozzy Osbourne* concert on the *Crazy Train* tour and *Motorhead* opened up for them. And now Peter and his band have been touring lately and are the opening act for *Motorhead*."

"It's funny how things come full circle. We sure had a great summer back in 1981," said John. "I wonder what ever happened to Eddie Burkoff."

"Mark told me many years later that he was married and divorced four times and he became a commercial ferry boat captain after he retired from the navy. He had to work until he was seventy to make all those payments that he had for alimony and child support."

"Serves him right," said Maria. "What about your friend Jeremy Laxter from *Vancouver* John? What ever happened to him?"

"Sadly, he died from *Aids* before it was cured," he said.

"That's too bad," said Maria.

John raised his glass to the crowd and gestured to everyone to toast with him.

"This is a toast to my two favourite cousins, Jeanette and Maria. May you live well but once you die, may you get to heaven half an hour before the devil knows you're there!" We all laughed. John was not the most diplomatic person in the crowd but he was a great cousin who made me laugh.

Nick came over next and said to us, "I hope you had a good birthday Mom and *Tante* Maria. It certainly was a lot of fun to hear the stories of your trip out west in your wild and crazy days," he said. "It sounded like you had quite the adventure in your younger days together."

"And we still are Nick, thanks," said Maria.

At the end of the day when everyone had left, Maria and I contemplated the day's events while sitting outside on my porch and watching the stars appear one by one up in the night sky. As

Maria lit up a cigarette and I had a glass of wine, I said to her, "Are you ever going to quit that nasty habit?"

"Hell No!" she said.

"What about swearing?"

"Fuck No! What about your wine? Are you ever going to give that up?" she asked me.

"Hell No!" I said.

"What about swearing?"

"Fuck No!" I said.

We laughed out loud about our silliness and watched a shooting star race across the night sky. I made a wish that the night would not end too quickly. I thought back to the time when Maria was kicked out of the house when we got back from our trip out west and she left to go to *Vancouver*. The years that she was away felt like lost years to me since we were out of touch with each other. Even though I felt that she was alright, I still had an uneasy feeling while she was away but I never really knew the total pain that she had gone through while she lived out there.

"I was glad when you decided to come back to *Ontario*. I missed you and felt really awful when you got kicked out of the house," I said. "The household was gloomy while you were gone and both Mom and Dad were miserable for a long time. It affected us all."

"Well, it was no picnic for me either. I am glad now that I met up with Larissa and she has been in my life ever since I contacted her many years ago," said Maria. "At least I can truly say I feel more at peace today because of that. I still feel bad though that I wasn't able to get that ring back to you like I promised Jeanette."

"That's okay," I said to her. "It's only a ring. I'm just glad that things have turned out better for you now. Mom had a feeling you either joined a biker gang or you were hanging out on the street corner waiting for customers when you were out there in *Vancouver*."

"Well, she had the right feeling alright," said Maria. "I only hung out with Rocco for a short while and after I got pregnant, he wanted me to have an abortion and become my pimp. I knew that's where I had to draw the line. The drugs, the sex and the easy money were all very lucrative but I knew better and got myself away from it, had my baby and gave her up to a good home."

"Thank *God* you did Maria," I commented. "Did you have a good day today?"

"Yes, I did," said Maria. "What about you?"

"Yes, me too," I said. "It was a great day worth remembering, as long as I can still remember!"

Even though it was a great day worth remembering, we were together for the last time. Maria passed away that night while in her sleep and I felt at peace for her. She had a hard life and made it difficult for herself most of the time. Our mother used to say, "Maria is her own worst enemy." She made choices in her life, as we all do and had to live with them. In the end though, I was glad that she admitted that the best choice was to keep a bit of paradise in your heart and be thankful for having something to hang onto.